JACK KNIFE

A pulse-pounding British crime thriller
with an astonishing twist

STEVE PARKER

Joffe Books, London
www.joffebooks.com

First published in Great Britain in 2023

Cover art by Nick Castle

ISBN: 978-1-83526-129-3

1975

Detective Inspector William Roach emerged from the sleek black Wolseley 6/80 police car, his shoes slapping onto the rain-soaked pavement. He pulled the collar of his woollen overcoat up to his ears, shielding his neck and face from the cold, biting wind. His trilby hat sat firmly atop his head, completing his detective ensemble.

He glanced up at an impenetrable blanket of grey clouds stretching as far as the eye could see. Cold raindrops pelted his face and he squinted against the gusts of wind that whipped around him, threatening to knock him off balance. Despite the thick coat and layers beneath, Roach still felt the chill seeping into his bones. He shuddered involuntarily, fighting to keep his teeth from chattering as he made his way towards the crime scene.

Detective Constable George Ford turned off the chromium-plated bell and the illuminated *Police* signs, his movements quick and efficient. He adjusted his flat cap and shrugged on his mac, determined to face the elements head-on. With a practiced hand, he reached into the back seat of the car and retrieved Roach's tan leather briefcase before joining his boss in the rain. Together, they stood on the pavement amid the roar of the A2 traffic. Roach surveyed the bleak landscape, the grey buildings in the distance blending seamlessly with the overcast sky. He couldn't help but feel a sense of foreboding, as if the dreariness of the surroundings was the backdrop to the crime that awaited them.

As they hopped over a low-level barrier and made their way across the patch of grass towards the crime scene, Roach spotted his sergeant, Danny Royce, waiting for them. Royce was a formidable man, with a flat nose and a face that still bore the scars of encounters with the notorious Richardson brothers back in the mid-sixties.

'Morning, sir.' Royce's voice was gruff and no-nonsense.

Roach nodded an acknowledgement, his attention already focused on the task at hand. As they approached the crime scene, he braced himself for the grim reality that awaited him. 'Morning, Danny. What delights do I have awaiting me, then?'

Royce flicked his head back toward the scene. 'Come and have a look. But mind how you go down this slope, boss. It's deadly.'

The two men gingerly navigated down a treacherous slope, clinging to each other for support on the slippery grass. As they finally reached the level ground, their breaths misted in the frigid air. In the distance, a group of five police officers huddled around a hastily constructed white tent surrounded by caution tape. The officers stationed at each corner shivered in the biting wind, while the fifth stood guard at the entrance, dutifully recording the purpose and identity of anyone who wanted to enter. Undeterred by the harsh weather, Roach and Royce trudged onwards towards the tent.

'Go on, then. What we got?' said Roach, trying to stop his teeth from chattering.

Royce sniffed back a small dewdrop on the end of his nose. 'Young girl. I'm guessing maybe eighteen — twenty, perhaps. She's naked and . . . eviscerated, guv.'

Roach stopped in his tracks. 'What?'

'Eviscerated. Her guts and stuff are—'

'I know what it means, Danny. Disembowelled. I was just a bit taken aback, that's all.' They resumed walking. 'How long since she was found?'

'About an hour or so, give or take. There's a forensic pathologist and a SOCO in there now having a look.' The scenes of crime officer was a fairly recent innovation for the Metropolitan Police, having been introduced in 1968 to replace the functions normally carried out at a crime scene by the CID. It was a challenge for Roach and Royce to stand back and allow a civilian to do what had previously been their job. But progress was the order of the day.

The tearing sound of retching came from the blind side of the tent. As they took two steps nearer, a man staggered into view on wobbly legs. He wiped his mouth with the back of his sleeve.

'Looks like the SOCO's giving it a break for a while,' said Royce.

'Can we go in, then?'

'Yeah. We can. Not sure you'll want to, though, guv. It's not nice.'

'I'm sure it's not. Still . . . it's the job, eh? Goes with the territory.'

The officer at the entrance to the tent held up his clipboard, pen at the ready. Roach held up his warrant card. 'DI Roach, senior investigating officer, and this is DS Royce.' He turned to DC Ford. 'Hang on here, George. Don't want too many inside.' DC Ford nodded.

The officer pulled back the flap to allow the two detectives inside. Roach nodded at him as he walked past.

Stepping warily inside the tent, Roach's eyes were drawn to the exposed legs of the victim, her lifeless body hidden from view by the hunched figure of the pathologist. The sombre air inside the tent was thick with the pungent stench of death, a sickly mixture of stomach acid, blood and decay that clung to Roach's senses like a suffocating blanket. It was a smell he knew all too well, a scent that had haunted him through years of attending morgues.

Despite the nausea that threatened to overwhelm him, Roach was relieved to note that the odour was not as overpowering as it could have been, an indication that the victim had likely been discovered soon after her demise. He silently thanked whatever stroke of luck had led to her being found before the smell of death had fully taken hold.

While he waited for the pathologist to acknowledge him, he scanned his memory for any nearby buildings he'd seen when he arrived. A hotel less than half a mile away . . . couple of office blocks roughly two miles further back. Did his killer work in one of them? Did his victim? Early days. One step at a time. He took his hat off, shook the water off it and coughed slightly.

The pathologist turned. 'Ah. Hello. I'm sorry. Engrossed, I'm afraid. And you are?' His accent was middle class. He didn't get up.

'Detective Inspector Bill Roach, and this is Detective Sergeant Danny Royce. And you?'

'Peter McKinnon. Forensic pathologist. Called to the scene by the SOCO. I'd be grateful if you two gentlemen would wait there for a moment or two. I'm just finishing up my preliminary exam and then we can chat.'

'Of course,' said Roach.

The pair stood in silence for a few minutes until McKinnon stood up. 'Right. Finished. For now. I'll know more once she's moved back to the mortuary. In the meantime, I can tell you that I think she was alive when our killer did this.'

'Alive?' said Roach. 'Why's that?'

As McKinnon moved aside, Roach caught sight of the girl and wished he hadn't. Her arms and legs, spattered with blood, were a chalky white colour. Her hair, ponytailed and blonde, was matted with blood. Her stomach was ripped open, and her intestines strewn around her torso. Her face was frozen in agony.

'Good God Almighty!' said Roach.

'Told you, guv,' said Royce.

'Yes,' said McKinnon. 'Dreadful. I haven't seen anything quite this bad before. Poor girl was only young. I estimate her to be about eighteen.'

However much he wanted to, Roach couldn't tear his eyes away. A hundred things ran through his mind. The most distressing was going to be telling her family their daughter had been murdered, and on top of that what had happened to her. No parent should hear that sort of news. He tried to snap out of it. 'A kid. For God's sake, she's just a kid.' He shook his head and looked up into the roof of the tent for a few seconds.

'She hasn't been dead for too long,' said McKinnon. 'It might be worth searching for your killer locally.'

Roach tore his gaze away from the girl. 'I've already thought of that,' he said, a touch brusquely. The CID may have lost their place to civilians at crime scenes but he was buggered if he was going to allow them to replace their detective skills completely. 'I'll get my people to check the local offices and that. How long do you think she's been dead? Rough guide.'

McKinnon drew in a deep breath. 'Three hours maybe. I've checked the times of the weather, and the rain started an hour and a half ago. The first police officer on scene reported only drizzle. Luckily for us, he was smart enough to cover her body with his mac. Kept her dry the best he could. Would've lost evidence if he hadn't.'

'Hmm,' said Roach. 'I'll thank him later. Do you have any evidence we can get started on at the moment?'

McKinnon shook his head. 'Well, no. Not forensic anyway. Not yet. I want to get her back so I can carry out a more thorough investigation. What I can tell you is this. Two things. The first is that cut was made skilfully. This looks bad because of the insides being outside, but it wasn't a frenzied job. She was cut cleanly by a scalpel and her innards carefully removed. Whoever did this knew what they were doing.'

'So, what then? A surgeon?'

'Can't be completely sure but, yes, most likely.'

Roach wrinkled his nose. 'You said the poor kid was alive when he did this?'

'I believe so, but I'm sure she would have died quickly after the incision was made. Shock first, blood loss next.'

'Small mercies,' said Roach. 'What's the second thing?'

McKinnon walked over to a small table in the corner of the tent, a standard prop for laying out anything that could be construed as evidence. He lifted up a brown paper evidence bag, unsealed.

'What's that?' said Royce. 'I can't see it properly in this light.'

McKinnon held it closer. 'It's a tape recorder. When we found it, it was inside a plastic bag and sealed with Sellotape — presumably to keep the rain off. I dropped it into one of our evidence bags ready for sealing and labelling. Thought you might want to have a listen to it first, though.'

'Where was it?'

'It was lying on her chest. First officer on scene said it was there when he arrived.'

'Her chest? Any idea why?'

'Not at all,' said McKinnon. 'But I suspect he wanted to be absolutely sure it was found.'

'You listened to it?' said Roach.

'I have.'

'And what's on it, then?'

'This . . .' McKinnon pressed the *play* button.

After a few seconds of hissy lead-in time, Roach recognised the opening bars. 'That's Bobby Darin, isn't it? "Mack the Knife." What the hell?'

'It's a sixty-minute tape,' said McKinnon. 'This is the only song on it. Both sides. I've fast forwarded it and the song's repeated over and over again.'

'Why that song?' said Royce.

McKinnon and Roach shrugged simultaneously.

'Maybe he's a fan,' said Roach.

'He has taste, then,' said Royce.

Roach scoffed. 'I've got a bad feeling this song is his way of introducing himself to the world.'

McKinnon sighed. 'I certainly hope not. Look, I'll have a report on your desk by five o'clock this evening.'

Roach nodded. 'Thank you.'

Roach put his trilby back on, and he and Royce stepped back out into the rain.

'What do you think, guv?' said Royce. 'Nasty, eh?'

Roach nodded slowly. 'This is not going to be the last we hear from our killer, Danny. I can feel it in my bones. He left that tape to announce his arrival. He's bloody taunting us. This is going to be a long and difficult chase.'

He had no idea the chase wouldn't end for nearly fifty years.

CHAPTER ONE

Present Day

William Roach spent the last few minutes of his eightieth year sitting in a small, dull bedroom. He hadn't told anyone. It didn't matter to anyone now. Soon, the clock would tick over past midnight and he would spend the first hours of his eighty-first birthday waiting for a woman he barely knew to die.

In the corner of the room, a small oil-filled radiator did a sterling job of warming the place just enough to be comfortable, but he still felt a little chilly. He stood up from the large comfortable chair he'd settled into. He reached for his walking stick and shuffled across the room to take a thin woollen blanket from on top of a dresser. Perks of old age, he mused. On his way back, he paused for a moment to look out of the only window and into the street below. Drops of rain tapped against the glass and he struggled to make out anything meaningful in the street. His eyes had long ago lost the sharpness they once had and now, looking out of the window, every streetlight had a gentle orangey halo around it. The streets themselves were no more than shiny black geometric shapes slick with rain. Somewhere in the distance, a dog barked a few times and the wail of a siren faded away into the distance.

Her name was Gillian Lake. She was ninety-three years old and had two children. Ronnie, her son, was living off-grid somewhere in New Zealand. He and his wife had given her three grandchildren, whom she had met only once. Her daughter, Casey, she'd had in her early forties. Her birth was touch and go and nearly killed Gillian, and it may have been for that reason that the women never really bonded. Casey Lake, now in her fifties, was married to her job as a police officer.

Gillian's husband, Clive, a man she had been married to for just shy of sixty-five years, had died suddenly ten years before. Casey, like Ronnie, rarely saw her mother and, in effect, Gillian was alone.

It had always upset Bill that people died without anybody being there to see them out: no family to hold their hands, no one to tell them that, whatever they did in their lives, someone loved them. That they were grateful for the things they had done for them and for the sacrifices they had made on their behalf. He was happy to be that missing someone, that missing person who should have made the journey to be here.

He turned away from the world outside and looked at the woman. In health, Gillian had been what Bill would have called a rake of a woman. She'd always been thin, almost painfully so, but it suited her. The last three months had seen her weight plummet further and she now reminded him of a tiny, frail bird about to fall out of its nest.

Leaning forward, he gently kissed her on the forehead before whispering in her ear that it was okay to go now, to be free of the pain and be with her Clive. He couldn't know if his words made a difference to her passing but he'd once read that hearing was the last thing to go on a dying person. He hoped it was true.

He sat himself back down in the comfortable chair and spent a few moments adjusting the woollen blanket over his body, making himself as comfortable as he could. He reached across and took Gillian's hand. The skin on her fingers was paper thin, barely concealing the frail little bones that were wracked with arthritis. Raised blue veins stuck out on the back of her hand, ripe and ready to burst. Her hand was icy cold to the touch. Her time was near. Her breathing, such as it was, was slow and laboured. She made a rasping sound with each breath.

Still holding her hand, Bill closed his eyes and eventually drifted off into an uncomfortable sleep.

At 3.27 a.m., Gillian Lake died.

CHAPTER TWO

Susan Johnson approached Gillian's room with a heavy heart, already bracing herself for the sight that awaited her. As soon as she laid eyes upon the still form of the elderly woman, she knew that death had claimed her. But it was Bill's motionless figure that gave her pause.

He sat in the chair, his body slumped forward, his mouth hanging open in a silent scream that mirrored the twisted expression of Gillian's lifeless face. The blanket that had once covered him lay forgotten in a heap at his feet. In the dimly lit room, it was difficult to tell whether he was still breathing or not, and a cold sense of dread settled over Sarah as she considered the possibility that he too had passed on.

Old Bill had become a familiar presence in Sarah's life at the Crown Woods Retirement Home, a beloved grandfather figure who had touched her heart with his gentle nature and quiet strength. The thought of losing him was unbearable, and she approached his unmoving body with a sense of trepidation, praying that he was still alive.

Bill was a kind man for whom nothing was too much trouble, a man who had always been there to listen to her when she brought her tales of woe into work with her. Car trouble? Bill advised her what the problem was likely to be, although his advice was dated to the late nineties, when he had last worked on fixing a car. Boyfriend trouble? Bill offered to sort him out, whoever he was and however big he might be. They both knew it was a gesture and not a promise he could keep. Money trouble? Susan never asked. Not once. But Bill helped her out — dropped her a hundred pounds here and there. He said he didn't need it, not at his age — might as well get some use out of it rather than let it sit there in the bank and, of course, he wouldn't tell a soul. There was no way he was ever going to drop Susan in it. She'd become the granddaughter he never had.

His thin and fragile hands were hidden within the deep pockets of his dressing gown. With gentle care, she reached out and lifted his right hand gently from the pocket, feeling the icy chill of his skin as she clasped his wrist, searching for a sign of life. Her fingers pressed against his delicate skin, seeking out the faintest hint of a pulse. As she felt the slow but steady beat beneath her fingertips, she released a soft sigh of relief.

Her attention then turned to the still form of Gillian, her heart heavy with the knowledge that she had already passed. She carefully stepped over Bill's outstretched legs and reached for the cold and withered wrist of the elderly woman. She knew even before she touched her that there would be no pulse. Still, she lifted Gillian's arm, feeling the stiff resistance of rigor mortis beginning to take hold, a sad reminder of the inevitable fate that awaited us all.

She knelt down in front of Bill and shook his hand gently.

'Bill,' she whispered. 'Bill.' She searched his face for some kind of movement. Bill started and in that second, her heart jumped.

Old Bill ran his tongue around his mouth a few times, taking off the build-up of white saliva in the corners, a mixture of spit and dead cells that had accrued during the night. He blinked a few times before turning toward Gillian and pulling himself upright. With some effort, he pulled himself out of the chair.

'Has she . . .'

'I'm sorry, Bill. She's gone.'

Bill nodded gently and patted Gillian's hand a few times before bending forward and kissing her on the forehead again. 'Safe journey, Gillian Lake. Safe journey.' He pulled her blanket up and rested it gently over her face.

'You okay, Bill?' said Susan.

He turned and gave her a weak smile. 'Course I am. It happens at our age. Can't do anything about it, can we?'

Susan shook her head. 'No. No, we can't. I'm sorry.'

'Don't be sorry, love. It's okay.'

Susan bent to pick up Bill's fallen blanket and draped it over his shoulders. She handed him his walking stick.

He nodded. 'Cold in here, girl. Any chance of a cuppa?'

Susan smiled. 'Of course. Let me lock up here and make the call to Dr Cooper and then I'll make you one. You want it in your room or in the dining room?'

Bill stopped for a second. 'Dining room, please,' he said, then ambled off along the corridor while Susan locked the door behind her.

CHAPTER THREE

As she made her way to the dining room, Susan spotted Bill already seated at a table that boasted a picturesque view of the lush garden beyond. A small group of residents clustered around him, their expressions a mix of concern and affection. The weight of yet another loss was clearly visible on his shoulders.

Despite their efforts to cheer him up, she could see that Bill was lost in thought, his gaze unfocused as he grappled with the pain of yet another loss. The residents knew better than to intrude upon his grief, but they couldn't help offering comforting words and gestures of sympathy, if only to remind him that he wasn't alone.

Susan felt a pang of sadness as she watched the scene unfold, knowing that this was just one of the many heart-wrenching moments that came with working in a care home. But she also felt a sense of pride in the residents, who had formed such a tight-knit community that they instinctively rallied around one another in times of need.

'You okay, Bill?' said Susan. 'Someone made you a tea?'

Bill looked up at her and shook his head. 'No. This lot are useless.' He winked at Madge. At ninety-one, she had now assumed Gillian Lake's crown as the oldest resident in.

'I offered you a cup,' Madge said, a slightly hurt expression on her face.

'I know you did, love, and I appreciate it. I do. But let's be fair . . . with the amount of wobble and shake on you, there wouldn't have been much left in the cup by the time it got to me, would there?'

She smiled and wagged a bony finger at him, the way an elderly grandmother would admonish a naughty grandchild.

'Where's your mug, Bill?' said Susan.

'In the cupboard over the sink,' he said. 'Where it always is. Or should be. That's where I put it last night.'

Susan reached up into the cupboard and pulled out Bill's favourite mug, an old beige tin cup with a faded Pepsi logo on both sides. She glanced at the inside of it and wrinkled her nose at the old brown tea stains that lined its walls. 'When did you last wash this, Bill?'

'Yesterday. I always wash it. Why?'

'It looks filthy.'

'It looks it, but it isn't. It's just stained. I like it stained. I think it has more of a real tea taste like that.'

'Why don't you get a new one? Just saying.'

'Nope. I like that one. I've had it for years. It's my lucky mug. Plus, everyone knows it's mine and not to touch it.'

'I don't think anyone would. Chances are they'd be ill.'

'Well, I'm not getting rid of it, and you better not either.' He gave her a little smile. 'Seriously. It's been with me for ever.'

Susan shook her head and checked the weight of the kettle before flicking on the switch. 'Okay, you're the boss. I just can't figure out why you haven't got botulism yet. Bloody miracle.'

* * *

'So, I don't need to worry about yer?' said Bill's friend Charlie. 'You're alright, then?' Charlie was the same age as Bill. Born and raised in London's East End, had been a resident for over eight years. He and Bill hit it off straight away and had been inseparable since their first meeting five years before, when Bill was admitted. Charlie's wife was dead some twenty-five years and his son had gone to New York for work. The son met and married a local girl, settled down and had a couple of kids. Apart from the occasional visit from his son and the grandkids, it had been a lonely twenty-five years. His other son, he saw a bit more. He'd come and visit Charlie in the home once or twice a year, but that depended on whether he was in or out of prison.

'Yeah, I'm alright, Charlie. Just brings me down a bit, y'know?'

'Yeah, yeah. Course it does. Must do.' Charlie took a loud slurp of his lukewarm tea. 'Look. You need to stop this, me old mate. Depressing, this is for yer.'

Bill nodded, uninterested in Charlie's advice, and glanced outside. The sky was a mix of angry grey and black clouds and the rain fell hard.

'Tea up, boys!' Susan walked over with two mugs of tea. One for Bill, one for Charlie. 'Made you another, Charlie? Figured you'd drink it.'

'And you figured absolutely right, my little angel,' Charlie said.

She was good at her job. Kept an eye on things. Kept an eye on them all. Tried to make their existence that little bit more palatable. She sat herself down at the table and pulled out half a packet of chocolate digestives from her tunic pocket.

'Oh, you are a sweetheart!' said Charlie. 'How'd you know I wanted a biccy?'

'When do you not want a biscuit?' Susan said.

'Can't argue with that, gel.' Charlie untwisted the packet before taking the top two biscuits out. 'Anyone else?'

'I'll have a couple, please,' said Bill.

'So, are you going to listen to Charlie and stop sitting with people when it's . . . y'know . . . their time?' said Susan.

Bill dunked his biscuit in his tea and shook his head. 'Nope.'

'Why not? It's not on you to see them out, Bill.'

'I know that. But someone has to. Most of the people in here are shoved in here by kids that don't want them, or they don't have any family to look after them, and then they're forgotten about. Literally forgotten about. Might get the odd Christmas or birthday card, one or two visits for half an hour at a time but that's about it. Someone needs to be there for them. It's only right. No one should die alone, is how I see it.'

'People have lives, though, Bill. They get busy raising their own kids. Work and all that. It's a busy world now.'

Bill scoffed. 'Funny how they all get unbusy when it's time to read the will, isn't it? Funny how they suddenly find a boatload of time to fight and bitch among themselves over who gets what, isn't it? Can't spare a couple of hours every month to see their old mum but can spend three months in court every day trying to get their grubby little hands on Mum or Dad's money.'

'Wow!' said Susan. 'I didn't know you felt quite so strongly about it. That's quite lovely.'

'Well. Makes me bloody sick, it does. At least my sitting with them as they die is one little act of kindness. Something their families don't often show them.'

'You can't say that about everyone, though.'

'I'm not.' He swigged his tea. 'But you gotta admit it's more often than not. Right?'

Susan nodded. 'I suppose so.'

'Anyway. I'm all right. Nothing to worry about. Let's talk about something else.'

'Yeah,' said Charlie. 'Let's talk about how I just dropped the last bit of me biscuit in me tea.' He fished around inside his cup and pulled out a small piece of soggy chocolate biscuit. He popped it in his mouth and licked the wet chocolate off his fingers.

'What's happening with your studies, Sue?' said Bill. 'How you getting along?'

'Yeah. Good. I'm just waiting to get my final marks to let me know if I've passed. Fingers crossed.'

'You'll be fine. You're a very smart cookie, lady. Very smart.'

Susan was in the final year of her studies to become a criminal forensic psychiatrist. When she first told Bill, he joked that all psychiatrists were criminal, given the amount of money they charged. Bill liked her. She never patronised him or the other residents, treated them as adult human beings. In return, Bill always stood up for her and encouraged her. He often thought of her as the granddaughter he'd never had.

'Of course I am, Bill. That's why I work for minimum wage. In here. With you lovely lot.'

'What is it you're studying to be again?' Charlie licked the last bits of chocolate off his fingers. 'I know you told me but the old brain's a bit scrambled these days. Can't even remember if I put me shoes on today. Did I?' He leaned back and looked at his feet. Susan and Bill looked under the table too. 'Yep. I did. Gonna be a good day today.'

Susan chuckled. 'Forensic psychiatrist.'

'Who is?'

'I am, Charlie. Me. I want to be. *May* be. Who knows until the result comes in?'

'Funny job, that is.'

'How so?' she said, folding her arms.

'Well, what d'you have to do? Go to a crime scene and write up reports about who you think may have done it and why, yeah?'

'Yeah,' said Bill. 'Spot on, Charlie. You've got it. Should have been one yourself.'

A grin spread across Charlie's face. 'I would've done, mate, but me typing's not up to scratch.' He imitated a two-finger typist.

'You'll be fine, Susan,' said Bill. 'Trust yourself a bit more.'

'You gonna go and work with Bill's old firm, then?' said Charlie. 'That the plan?'

Bill shook his head.

'The Met?' said Susan. 'I don't know, to be honest. I'd like to, yes, but I'll go where they have openings, I guess.'

'Try for the Met, luv,' said Bill. 'Best of the bunch. They catch everyone in the end and they need clever people like you, for sure.'

'Thank you, Bill. Okay, look, I can't sit chatting with you two old buggers all day,' Susan said, getting up. 'I'll get in trouble. Work to do. Bedpans to change, medicines to give.' She picked up Bill and Charlie's mugs and headed toward the sink. 'You sure you're alright, Bill?'

'I'm fine, love. Honestly. Look, before you go, what time is Dr Cooper getting here? D'you know?'

'Soon as he's finished his morning surgery. Probably about midday, I would think.'

'You want me there?'

'See what he says, Bill. You were the last person to see her alive, so he might want to ask you a few questions. Usual stuff. That alright?'

'Yeah. No worries. Give me a shout when he arrives.'

With that, Susan gave everyone a big smile and breezed out of the dining room.

'Lovely girl,' said Bill.

'She is that,' said Charlie. 'She is that. Not like that miserable bag of bones, Jackie Draper. Fuck her halfway to hell and back.'

Bill laughed. 'Rather you than me, mate.'

'Chance'd be a fine thing at my age,' said Charlie.

The two men burst into laughter as a loud rumble of thunder shook the windows.

CHAPTER FOUR

Susan tapped on Bill's door and entered when he called her in. 'Bill. Dr Cooper's here. Says he'll have a quick word with you, if that's okay?'

Bill reached for his walking stick and hauled himself up from his chair. He took a second or two to find his balance. 'Where is he? Is he with her?'

Susan nodded. 'He's only just got here. Went straight to her room. There's no rush. Take your time.'

Bill wandered out of his room and pulled the door closed behind him. He shuffled along the corridor to Gillian Lake's room, five doors along from his. The door hung half-open and Susan stepped inside without hesitation. 'Bill's here, Doc.' Her voice carried through the quiet of the room.

Dr Sean Cooper turned to greet them, his form silhouetted against the window as he stood by the side of Gillian's bed. In contrast with the sombre atmosphere of the room, there was a certain cheerful kindness in the doctor's features. He was a portly man in his forties, dressed in a manner that could only be described as 'countrified'. His tweed jacket and corduroy trousers, paired with well-polished brown brogues, seemed more at home on a country estate than in a London retirement home. Wire-rimmed glasses perched on his nose and the scars of childhood acne were still visible on his cheeks. He looked more like an old-fashioned country vet than a modern-day doctor.

For Bill, accustomed to the slick and polished appearance of London GPs, Dr Cooper's appearance was a stark contrast. He couldn't help but notice the eccentricity of the man's dress sense and the distinct air of nostalgia that seemed to cling to him. He wasn't overly fond of the doctor.

'Hello, Doctor. How are you?'

'I'm fine, Bill, thank you. You well?'

'Mustn't grumble.' He put himself in the corner of the room, giving him a good view of the doctor and of Gillian Lake.

'You stayed with her last night? Is that right?'

'Yep.'

'How did she seem to you?'

'A bit better than she does now, that's for sure.'

Susan smiled and covered it with a hand.

'I'm sure she did,' said Cooper. No sense of humour there. 'What I mean is, did she seem distressed in any way?'

Bill shrugged. 'I don't think so, no. She was asleep. Been asleep for the best part of two days. That's why I went to sit with her.'

'How d'you mean? I don't understand.'

'You don't have to be a doctor to know when someone's on their last knockings, do you? I've seen enough people dying in my time to know when the man with the scythe's sniffing around.'

The doctor nodded. 'Of course. You were a policeman.'

'Mm-hm.'

'Can you remember what time you last saw her alive?'

'Just after midnight. I spoke a few words to her and held her hand. That was it.'

'I'm not being critical, Bill, but did you not think to call one of the staff?'

'For what? What could they do?'

'Call an ambulance, perhaps.'

Bill shook his head at him. 'What good would that do? She was ninety-three, for Chrissakes. So, they whip her off to hospital and keep her going. Pump her heart, wire her up, stick tubes in and out of her and leave her alone in the ICU for a fortnight where she dies all on her own. Just machines around her. Or, she lives . . . the hospital boot her out because they need the bed, she comes back here and has to sit in her own piss and misery for the next couple of years before dying anyway. How cruel is that? Sometimes it's best to just let people go.'

Dr Cooper cocked his head. 'It's a tough call, but Bill, it's not your call to make. This isn't the first time you've done this, is it?'

Bill pulled himself as straight as he could. His fingers curled around his walking stick. 'Excuse me? Done what?'

'This. What we've just spoken about.'

'What? Been kind to someone? Is that it? Being human? Listen . . . I haven't done anything wrong. I've not commit-ted a crime, have I? No. I've just been there for someone as they pass. It's called compassion. You lot want to give it a go sometime. It used to be popular back in my day.' His voice trembled and he wobbled about just enough for Susan to take his arm and steady him.

'It's okay, Bill. I'm sure Dr Cooper wasn't having a go at you.' She turned to Cooper and fired daggers at him. 'Were you, Dr Cooper?'

Cooper looked a bit taken aback by Bill's little attack on him and his profession. 'What? No. God . . . No . . . I was just saying—'

'Well, think before you say, Doc,' said Bill. 'It came across wrong. Sorry if I got the wrong end of the stick. Sorry.'

'It's okay, Bill. I know you didn't mean it.' Dr Cooper picked up his bag and turned to Susan. 'Well, we know that she died between, say, half past midnight and when you found her this morning at . . . what? Eight, did you say?'

'Eight thirty. She was my first call this morning.'

'Did you get up in the night, Bill?' said Cooper. 'For a leak, perhaps?'

Bill shook his head. 'No. New tablets. Slept like a baby.'

'Okay, time of death somewhere between twelve thirty and eight thirty. No suspicious circumstances.'

Susan nodded. 'Amount of tablets she was taking, she did well to get this far. Heart problems, liver, kidney . . . Amazing really.'

'Hmm,' said Dr Cooper. 'Sudden, but not entirely unexpected.'

'You finished with me, Doc?' said Bill.

'Yes, Bill. Sorry to call you here.'

'Not a problem. Susan, I'm going downstairs to make another cuppa, you want one?'

She glanced at her watch. 'Sorry, Bill. No time.'

'Doc? You want one?'

'Please, Bill. A quick cup would be nice.'

'I'll get the kettle on.' Bill turned and shuffled out of the door and along the corridor, making his way toward the lift.

* * *

'I'll leave you it then, Doctor,' said Susan. 'I'll write up my report later and email it across to you as usual, okay?'

Dr Cooper held up his hand. 'Have you got a minute, Susan?'

'Mm-hm. What's up?'

'We're going to have to stop him from doing this.'

'What? Why?'

'Well, he doesn't let staff know, for a start.'

'He doesn't have to, Doc. We know when these people are dying on us. They're seen and made comfortable by the nurse here, Mrs Lennon. She saw no point in sending Mrs Lake to the hospital. And, as Bill said, there was no point.'

Dr Cooper sighed. 'Mrs Dunbar needs to be careful, is what I'm saying.'

'Well then, with respect, Doctor, you need to take it up with her. As far as I'm concerned, Bill is providing a service. A kindness. That's a very rare commodity these days. So, unless he's breaking any rules of the home or committing some sort of crime, we're all more than happy for him to do this. Look, I'm sorry. I have to go. Busy, I'm afraid.'

'Have the family been informed?'

'I believe so. Mrs Dunbar would do that. A phone call, probably. I know she left a message for the daughter last night to say that her mum had taken a nasty turn and to get here if she could. I guess she couldn't.'

Cooper nodded. When Susan had left the room, he turned to look at Gillian Lake. After a moment, he pulled the sheet back over her face.

CHAPTER FIVE

'Your tea's on the table, Doc,' said Bill.

Cooper gave him a smile and weaved around the tables. He dropped his case, heavy with papers, medicines and the odd piece of essential equipment, onto the chair next to him before sitting down.

'You alright, Doc?' said Charlie.

'Tired, Charlie. Worn out. I think this is more of a young man's game.'

'Leave off! You're still a baby. Wish I was your age.'

Cooper pulled his mug of tea toward him. 'I take your point. Still, I can't race about like I used to.'

'None of us can,' said Bill. 'Get your tea down your neck.'

'How are you doing, Charlie?' asked Cooper. 'When's your next visit to the surgery? I need to check on your heart.'

'Dunno off the top of me head, Doc, but I'm happy to whip me shirt off now, if you like.' Charlie started to undo the buttons on his cardigan.

Cooper smiled. 'Surgery appointment will be fine, thank you.'

'Tch. Would have saved us both a bit of time.' Charlie did his buttons back up.

'You all right, Bill?' said Cooper. 'You seem a bit . . . edgy. Something happened?' Bill pulled a grimy handkerchief out of his pocket and wiped the little drop of snot that hung precariously from the tip of his nose. He sniffed at the same time as he wiped. Putting his hanky back, he nodded toward the main office, the office hours home of Mrs Julie Dunbar, the owner of Crown Woods.

Slowly, Cooper turned to look, then spun back around. 'Draper, eh? Still not gone?'

Bill shook his head. 'Got it made here, ain't she? Dunbar owns the place, but Draper rules the roost. Nasty mare won't go unless she's carted out in a box, I reckon.'

Charlie put his mug down. 'Don't know why you worry about her, Bill. She's just a bully in a dress. Tell her to piss off if she starts.' He made a point of staring at Draper through the glass window of the office.

'Yes, Bill,' said Cooper. 'Don't let her upset you. Take no notice of her.'

'It's not that easy. Bitch has got her claws into me and she's not letting go. Makes my life a bloody misery, she does.'

'You're too nice, mate,' said Charlie. 'That's your problem.'

'Yeah, well. It's not that easy for me these days. I'm not what I used to be. Don't have the strength to stand up to her. Don't have the brainpower either. I get . . . muddled when she starts on me.' Bill looked over at the office and saw Draper staring back at him. He felt his stomach lurch. An old feeling of excitement, a flash of the old days when he faced down many people who would do him harm. He never lost a fight. Not once. But now, age and infirmity had robbed him of that confidence and ability.

Dr Cooper drained his mug. 'Gentlemen, I have to go. Thank you for the tea. Bill, I'll see you in a couple of weeks, no doubt. Charlie, see you in the surgery.'

Both men waved him off and watched him walk past Mrs Dunbar's office before pulling open the main door to the street. As the door swung shut behind him, Mrs Dunbar walked into the room. Bill spotted her and waved. She smiled and waved back before joining them both.

'Morning, Bill,' she said, sitting down opposite him.

'Morning.'

'How are you?'

'Tired and achy. Those chairs are not the most comfortable.'

Mrs Dunbar nodded. 'I know. I saw Dr Cooper leaving. You two have a chat?'

'Yeah. Nothing special. Just wanted to know if I could tell him exactly when she died. Wants it for his notes.'

'Yes, of course. Listen, I got a message from Gillian's daughter early this morning. She's coming in at the end of the week. She wants to have a chat with me.'

Bill sat upright. 'What about?'

'I don't think she's particularly happy that her mother died . . .'

Bill pulled a face at her. 'I'm sure she's not.'

'You know what I mean. She's not happy that she died so suddenly. And, according to the message I got, she's looking to have a post-mortem done.'

Bill narrowed his eyes. 'Is she now? Not sure that will happen. I mean, she died within forty-eight hours of seeing her GP and, if I recall, a PM isn't needed in that case. And especially for someone of that age.'

'I'm not sure. I'll have to speak with Dr Cooper about that. Anyway, you'll be around, won't you?'

Bill nodded.

'Good.'

'Good? Why good?'

'Well, she knows you were the last person to see her alive and probably just wants to ask you if she said anything before she died.'

'Like what? "Tell my daughter, *Thanks for never coming to see me. Everything I've ever owned is now yours and the cash and jewellery is under the floorboards.*" That sort of thing?'

Mrs Dunbar chuckled. 'Now, now, Bill. There you go with the cheekiness again.'

'Tell me I'm wrong.'

Mrs Dunbar nodded. 'I wish I could. You're most likely right but let's wait and see, shall we?'

He nodded again before taking a sip of his tea. 'When is she coming, again?'

'Toward the end of the week. She's going to call and confirm later today once she knows her diary.'

'*Knows her diary*? Who says stuff like that? I don't think we're going to get on at all.'

'Well, try to, Bill. She sounded very busy, and we don't know about her life.'

'We can all sound busy. That's not difficult, is it?' He didn't wait for an answer. 'Just let me know when you want me. Not like I'm going anywhere.' Mrs Dunbar walked back to her office, leaving Bill shaking his head.

'You all right?' said Charlie. 'Seem a bit upset, mate.'

'No, I'm fine. It is what it is. If she wants it done, so be it. That's it. It's nothing to do with me, is it?'

'No. It's not. It was her mum. Wonder why she wants it done?'

'That's easy. Her mum died unexpectedly. I mean, I know she was as clapped out as the rest of us, but she was doing okay a few days ago and then, *pfft*! Gone.'

Charlie nodded. 'Yep, it was quick. She had heart problems, didn't she?'

'Yeah. And a boatload of other stuff too. Age. Odds were against her.'

'Probably the old ticker gave out.'

'More than likely.'

Charlie got up from his chair. 'What d'you say to another cuppa?'

Bill pushed his mug forward. 'I'd say, "Come here, you little beauty." Ta.'

Charlie chuckled as he walked over to the kettle.

'What d'you make of him, Charlie?' said Bill.

'Who's that?' Charlie filled up the kettle.

'The doc. Cooper.'

'The doc? Nice enough bloke. Why's that?'

'It's nothing.'

'Well, it's something ain't it? You wouldn't have asked otherwise, would you?'

Bill chuckled softly. 'Forget it.'

'Nope. Come on . . . out with it.'

Bill took a chocolate digestive from a small flowery plate and dunked it into what remained of his first cup of tea. 'Look . . . it's nothing. Just a thought.'

Charlie sat down while the kettle boiled. 'Christ, it's like pulling bloody teeth with you. Tell me!'

'You won't like it.'

'Try me.'

Bill nodded. 'It's just that . . . I've noticed that whenever he comes here to do his rounds, people seem to . . .' He left the words hanging for a couple of seconds. Too long for Charlie.

'What? What is it?' he said.

'Die. They seem to die within a couple of days of him being here.'

Charlie pushed himself back in his chair. 'What?'

'Have you not noticed?'

'Nope. Never even occurred to me.'

'Well, it has to me.'

'Oh, come on, Bill. Cooper's a good man. That's not his game.' He sat forward again. 'You're not serious, are you?'

Bill pushed away his mug and picked up his walking stick, resting on the chair next to him. 'No. Don't worry about it.' With one hand on his walking stick he pressed his other onto the table and forced himself to a standing position.

'Where you going? You can't just chuck that out into the air and walk off, you old sod.'

Bill twisted himself around, grimacing at a pain in his knee. 'I said you wouldn't like it. You don't. Let's just leave it at that, Charlie. It's probably my imagination, that's all. Rambling thoughts of an old man.'

'Or . . . Or it might be the old instinct kicking back in.'

Bill threw his friend a *don't take the piss* look.

'I'm serious, Bill. I dunno. Look . . . the kettle's boiled. Sit down and let's talk about it. I mean, what if you're onto something? You're probably not, but what if you are? What if Cooper's been doing a Shipman? I mean, that old doc killed, what, three hundred of his old wrinkly patients before they caught onto him, didn't he? Proper serial killer, that one.'

Bill snorted. 'Not my idea of a serial killer. Cosying up to old people, getting them to change their wills in his favour and then killing them off is a cowardly thing to do, if you ask me.'

'I agree. It is. But he did it. How do we know that Cooper ain't at it?'

Bill shrugged. 'Let it go, Charlie. I was being stupid. He couldn't get away with it these days. Lot's more safeguards in place because of Shipman.'

Charlie nodded. 'Still. If you're even thinking it, then there's a good reason. Have you mentioned it to anyone?'

'No. Apart from you, that is.'

'Don't you think you should?'

'What do I say? I'm an old man with a fuzzy brain, diabetes, a bit of dementia and Addison's disease.'

'What've diabetes and Addison's got to do with it? Don't affect your brain and your thinking, do they?'

'Not supposed to, but who knows?'

'You do, you silly sod. Dementia and old age affect your thinking, I'll grant you, but we've all got our fair share of that, ain't we?'

Bill smiled. 'Yeah. We have.'

'So are you going to — Oh! Head's up. Draper's on her way over. Stand by yer beds.'

Bill watched her approach. He knew the walk. Cocky. She'd start on him. Him and dozens of others. The day was young.

'Morning, you pair of old farts. Still alive, then?'

'Sod off, Draper!' said Charlie. 'Shouldn't you be at home beating that pack of wolves you call kids?'

Draper glared at him. 'You know what, Charlie? I should. But it's more fun to come in here and make your lives a little bit more miserable than they already are.'

Charlie stood up. 'Why'd you take a job in a care home? No jobs in the sewers these days? Khmer Rouge stopped recruiting?'

Bill winced.

'Who?' she said.

'Khmer Rouge. Mob of Cambodian commies back in the seventies. Nasty bunch that killed about one and a half million people. Executed them.'

'Oh! So, you're comparing me to them?'

'There's no comparison, love,' said Charlie. 'You're a sight more horrible. Maybe that's what you should do . . . stop them little sods of yours terrorising and thieving anything that's not nailed down.'

Draper stood facing Charlie, legs slightly apart. Bill could see that the back of her neck was red. 'You saying my kids should be killed? Don't you say that, Charlie boy, or you'll regret it.'

'Yeah? Well, I won't be the only one that regrets you having sprogs, will I?'

She spun on her heels, turning to face Bill. He was an easier target. 'And how's the resident copper, then? Always lovely to see the filth. Makes it easier to mop it up.'

Bill looked into her face. Jackie Draper was in her mid-fifties, thin as a rake and ugly as sin. Pockmarks riddled her cheeks and a spider's web of veins, a gift from all the alcohol she'd drunk over her wretched lifetime, lined her pig nose. She'd taken drugs from her early teens and added alcohol in her late teens through to the present day. She had five feral kids from four fathers, all of whom did a runner. Homeless twice and on the game once, life certainly hadn't been kind to Draper. She didn't give a jot about anything and cared for nothing and no one. Except her kids.

'Oi, oi, don't start on him!' said Charlie. 'He's done nothing to you. Leave him alone.'

'Aw, look at that, copper,' said Draper. 'Your girlfriend's sticking up for you. That's so sweet.'

'Get lost, Draper!' Bill snapped. 'You're no good.'

'Oooh! Bill gets a backbone!' Draper sneered. 'Except, you're . . . crying. Boo-hoo.'

Bill wiped at his eyes instinctively. 'I'm not crying. It's age. My eyes just water.'

'Course they do, love. You keep telling yourself that.' She turned back to Charlie. 'Got a tissue on you? I've made your girlfriend cry.' She walked away chuckling to herself, leaving Charlie and Bill fuming.

'Don't take any notice, Bill. She's just a nasty, twisted cow.'

Bill stood watching her through blurry vision. He wiped at his eyes again and nodded at his friend. 'I'm going back to my room. I don't want to be anywhere she is.'

'You're right, mate. I'm going to go watch TV in my room. You want to come? You're welcome to.'

'No thanks, Charlie. I've got some bits to do. Cheers, though.'

'Well, you know where I am if you change your mind. If not, see you later.'

Bill nodded and shuffled off to the corridor to take the lift.

CHAPTER SIX

Bill pushed open the door to his room and made his way over to his dressing table. He stood there for a moment or two, looking at the carefully arranged bits and bobs that were all that remained of his life. Once, he had lived in a four-bedroom house in Bexhill, close to the sea. He'd never married but had one child, a boy by the name of Tony who he hadn't seen in many years. Neither father nor son were particularly interested in each other. Bill wasn't the fatherly kind, but the idea of a son, someone to follow in his footsteps, appealed to him. The boy's mother, a prostitute Bill knew from his old job, initially wasn't interested in playing happy families. She told him she would have the child if that was what he wanted, but it would be on him to be the parent. Bill gave it a go, but his work demanded too much time from him.

The relationship didn't last and, when Bill made the mistake of questioning if he was the father during an argument, she disappeared with the child. He thought about searching for them, but his career was taking off and he figured the mother would have reached out if she had wanted him involved. He'd considered looking for them on more than a few occasions, but his career had been going well and he'd figured that if she wanted him playing any part of her life she would have been in touch. It was best to let sleeping dogs lie. So, he went to work and tried to forget.

And then, one day, the boy showed up on his doorstep, now a young man of eighteen. His mum had thrown him out. Bill took him in and, over the course of a few years, they got to know each other. He showed an interest in his father's work and Bill was happy to teach him some things that would help him later in life. All was going well until they had one argument too many and Tony walked out — this time, never to return.

After that, Bill never got close to anyone. He made a point of it. He liked his own company and worked best on his own and, while that suited him at the time, now, in his dotage, life was not as he'd expected.

Coming from a four-bedroom house to just one room made it difficult to choose what to bring with him. He had a faded, torn photograph of his father, John, taken when the man was twenty-one years old. Bill had a few memories of him, but not many. He vanished when Bill was six years old and was never seen again.

There were no photos of his mother, Elaine. Every memory of her was carefully omitted, as if her presence had been erased from his life. Bill detested the woman, who had quickly replaced his father with Gerald, a mild-mannered man who tried and failed to win Bill's affection. He couldn't understand why his father had gone and why his mother replaced him so quickly. The neighbours never liked her and would whisper about how she had likely buried him in her backyard or chopped him up in the basement, waiting until she could dispose of the body at the local waste tip. Neighbours loved to gossip.

A box of tissues, a comb, a brush and a family-size bag of Maltesers were the only other items that adorned the top of the dresser. He reached into his dressing gown pocket, pulled out his diabetes injection kit and placed it carefully next to his brush.

A tap on the door startled him. His first reaction was that Draper had come to torment him some more.

'Bill? It's Susan.'

He breathed a sigh of relief. 'Susan? Yes. Come in. Please.'

She poked her head around the door and gave him a big smile. 'Hiya. Just thought I'd pop in. I bumped into Charlie and he said that Draper had had a pop at you.'

Bill nodded. 'Bitch of a woman.'

Susan stepped inside and pulled the door to. 'Can't argue with that. She is bloody horrible.'

Bill ambled over to his chair, lowered himself in and sighed. 'Why can't we just get rid of her?'

'We've been over this. Shortages. Do you know how difficult it is to get staff these days? Course you do. It's not the first time we've spoken about this, is it? No. We're stuck with her for the foreseeable future, I'm afraid.'

'I don't understand why she's never been pulled up about it. Her attitude is disgusting.'

Susan crossed the room and pulled back the curtains. Bill squinted as the light hit his eyes. 'Again. Can't argue with that, but Mrs Dunbar isn't one for discipline. She's too nice and she knows Draper needs the job. She has kids.'

'Kids? They're not kids. More like rabid little rats. What are they? Teenagers? In their twenties? They should be going out to keep her, not lazing around shoving drugs in their arms. Useless sods.'

Susan laughed. Bill loved that little chuckle she did. It made him feel happy, and there was little in this world that brought happiness these days.

'Did you take your medicine?' she said.

'Which one? I've got too bloody many.'

'For your diabetes.'

'Oh, yeah. Took that this morning.'

'When?'

'When what?'

'When did you take your medicine?'

Bill shrugged. 'I can't remember. This morning.'

Susan opened the kit box and held the syringe up to the light. 'Okay. It's empty. I guess you did.'

'Of course I did. Would I lie to you? The prettiest, nicest person in here?' He smiled wryly.

'Flattery won't work, Bill. You know that. I just have to be sure you've taken it, that's all. If I don't, I get into trouble and you . . . well, I don't know what will happen to you, but it probably won't be good.'

Bill nodded and let out a long sigh.

'You okay?' she said.

'What? Hmm. Tired.'

'I'm not surprised. Sitting in a chair all night probably isn't good for you. I bet you hardly slept at all, did you?'

'It was okay, I suppose. I've had worse in my time.'

She smoothed out a little crease at the bottom of his unslept-in bed. 'I'm sure you have. Must have been hell in the First World War.'

'Oi! Cheeky. I'm not that bloody old.'

'What's bothering you, Bill? And don't just say it's Draper.' She parked herself on the edge of his bed and took his hand. 'Something is. Do you want to talk?'

Bill looked up at her and sniffed. 'I'm alright, love. It is just her, that's all. She makes everyone's life a bloody misery. This used to be a nice place before she turned up. Been a nightmare since then.'

She patted his hand. 'I know. Just try not to think about her too much. Stay away from her when you see her and don't talk to her. That's the best way to deal with her.'

'You know what?'

'No. What?'

'I've met all sorts in my life . . . good'uns, bad'uns and every stripe in between. But of all those people I've met, I can honestly say I hated none of them. Not one. Draper? She's the first. I despise her. If I was only thirty years younger—'

'Bill. Stop it. You'll set yourself off again. Last thing I want is you having a heart attack.'

Bill laughed. 'You're alright, girl. I'm not going any-where just yet. You can count on that.'

'Good. You and Charlie are the only thing that cheers me up when the leathery old cow has had a go at me too.'

Both of them laughed.

* * *

Outside in the hallway, her back pressed up against the wall and her ear craned toward the slightly open door, Jackie Draper shook her head.

CHAPTER SEVEN

Bill lifted the net curtain hanging limply from his window to the world and tutted to himself. Still, the rain fell steadily. He watched an ignorant car driver choose not to slow down as he drove through a puddle and soaked the legs of a young woman walking along the pavement.

He was tired. Sitting with a dying woman and sleeping awkwardly on a chair, albeit a comfortable one, had taken its toll on him. There were things to do, though. Today was shopping day and he ran a few errands for a couple of the residents who could not get about for themselves. It was about the only thing that he looked forward to these days. That, and the conversations he had with Susan and Charlie.

He'd often pondered how different his life may had been if he'd settled down, if things hadn't gone bad with his son's mother and if he'd seen anything of him growing up. Maybe he wouldn't feel so lonely. Maybe he would. His little shopping trips gave him the chance to get out and converse with people whose sole focus wasn't on what ailments they had and what medicines they were taking for them. It was good to chat to shop staff who, if they weren't too busy, would spend just a minute or two talking to him about trivialities and the state of the world in general. It wasn't much in the way of conversation, but it was something.

Before dropping the curtain back down, he glimpsed at his car parked in its usual place and debated momentarily whether or not he should take it. It was a ten-year-old Nissan automatic; his legs weren't as strong as they used to be and constantly change gears around town had proved exhausting. Also, the fact that he couldn't feel the pedals as well as he used to had led to him stalling the car far too often. Other drivers had been far from patient and the constant tooting of their horns at his predicament had been far too stressful. An automatic car had been the obvious solution.

The problem he had now was different. Over the last two years or so, his eyesight had got worse, as had his co-ordination. Dr Cooper had suggested that perhaps it was time to call it a day on the driving front and consider getting himself a cab if he wanted to go out and about. Bill knew the doctor was most likely right, but it didn't sit well with him. His car was the last real nod he had to his independence. To have to give that up was a step he wasn't quite ready to take. Age was proving to be a trial.

As he peered out the window, the raindrops splattering against the glass, Bill sighed. He had been planning on walking to the corner shop for his daily newspaper, but the inclement weather had other ideas. He knew he was getting older and his mobility wasn't what it used to be, but he was determined to maintain his independence as long as possible, dogged in his determination to keep going, to keep living his life on his own terms for as long as he possibly could.

The weather made his mind up for him: he'd take the car. But he'd have to take it slow on the roads. He knew how to drive, of course, but he wasn't as confident as he used to be. He often wished that someone would invent a magnetic plate, similar to 'L' plates but with a graphic of a bent-over old person on it that would let other drivers know the car was being driven by an elderly person, perhaps inspire a little bit of patience and consideration.

He spent the next fifteen minutes getting himself dressed and another five minutes checking he had everything he needed. Wallet and keys were the most important, and these he kept in a specific place so that his ailing memory didn't have to work any harder than it already was.

Satisfied he had everything, he decided to call on another resident, Peter Lord, to see if he fancied a ride into town. Peter was often up for a lift into town but Bill figured the weather would most likely put him off. He'd ask anyway. He closed the door behind him and tottered off toward the lift.

Peter Lord's modest little room was on the ground floor of the building and Bill would have to pass by Mrs Dunbar's office. He hoped that Draper would be elsewhere. Anywhere would do, just not in Dunbar's office.

As the lift doors slid open, his heart skipped a beat. Draper was there. So was Susan. It didn't take a body language expert to realise that Draper was laying into Susan. Draper's arms were flailing around and the look on her face could have dropped a charging elephant in its tracks. All that and the muffled shouting told him that there was a good chance that Draper had somehow overheard his and Susan's earlier conversation.

For a moment, he debated whether to storm into the office to defend Susan, but he quickly judged from her stance that she was holding her own against this vicious witch of a woman. His interference would likely make things worse.

As he shuffled toward the office, he caught Draper's eye. He saw her take a deep breath and her face scowled even deeper. Following Draper's glare, Susan turned her head. She nodded Bill onward. This wasn't an argument for him.

As he reached Peter's door, Draper's shouting suddenly became clearer. He turned to see Susan storming out of the office, leaving Draper to rant to an empty room. He hung his head and tapped on the door.

Peter Lord was a smartly dressed old boy in his eighties who took great pains to keep himself as healthy and fit as he could. A two-mile run every day helped him keep his weight down and his heart rate where it should be. He had one of those cheerful faces that lit up whenever he was pleased to see someone, and Bill caught the full beam of his radiant smile. 'Morning, Bill! Come in, come in!'

Bill shook his head. 'I'm not stopping, Pete. I'm going into town and wondered if you fancied it. Weather's a bit ropey, I know, but we should be able to park in the shopping centre.'

Peter nodded. 'Wasn't planning on going out today, mate. Nothing I need. But if you're stuck for a bit of company, I'm up for it. We can grab a cake and a cuppa at Greggs, yeah?'

'I've got a few things to pick up but, yeah, sounds like a plan. I'll go and warm the car up. Meet you in a couple of minutes.'

Peter grabbed a coat from the hallway rack and started to slip it on. 'No point hanging on, is there? Coat's on. Wallet in my pocket . . .' He quickly checked to make sure. 'Yep. All good. Greggs, here we come.'

Together, they made their way along the corridor toward the main doors.

'Hey, up,' said Peter. 'The Wicked Witch of Everywhere's in the office.'

'Hmm. Been there a while. Surprised you didn't hear her hollering and hooting.'

Peter gave Draper a cheery wave alongside one of his radiant smiles. It was only going to annoy her even more, but Peter wasn't one to change his ways simply because she didn't like it. He chuckled when she glared at him through the glass.

'Hollering and hooting, eh? Who's stuck the company pen up her arse today, I wonder?'

Bill gave a little chortle. 'That would be Susan. And me, I think?'

Peter turned to his friend. 'What've you two been up to, then?'

'We lost Gillian last night.'

'What?' Peter stopped walking.

'Hmm. She died in her sleep. It was her time.'

Peter nodded slowly. 'I'm sorry to hear that. She was lovely, old Gillian. Comes to us all, mate. Were you with her? S'pose you was.'

'Yeah.'

They started walking again.

'Anyway,' said Bill. 'I was in the dining room having a cuppa with Charlie and then Draper came in. She started straight in, didn't she? Wicked bitch she is.' He glanced back. Draper was still giving them both the hard stare.

'I went back to my room. Susan came in to see if I was okay and we started having a laugh together. You know how we are. Anyway, I've got a feeling Draper overheard us and that's why she tore into Susan. Can't think of any other reason she'd have a go at her. It's not like she's her supervisor or anything.'

'What did Susan do?'

Bill pushed the door open and instinctively pulled his head into his shoulders as protection from the rain, even though they were both still under the entrance cover.

'I think she stood up to her. She's sick to death of the shrew, just like the rest of us.' For some reason, Bill stuck his hand out to feel the rain on his upturned palm before quickly withdrawing it.

Peter smiled at him. 'Still raining then, is it?'

Bill nodded slowly. 'Bit silly, wasn't it?'

'No. You're alright. Force of habit, eh? I heard you coppers aren't big fans of the rain. Am I right?'

Pulling his collar up around his neck, Bill carefully negotiated the kerb and stepped tentatively into the road. 'Bloody right, we're not. No copper worth his salt would be caught in the rain.'

Peter laughed. 'Good man.' He followed Bill across the car park and the two men creaked and groaned their way into their seats. After a bit of huffing and puffing, they managed to get their seat belts on.

'You know what, Bill . . .' Peter's voice was serious. 'If they don't do something about Draper and the way she treats people, I can see someone dying of a heart attack from her constant bullying.'

Bill started the car and turned to face his passenger. 'Knowing my bloody luck, it'll be me.'

Peter sniffed and fumbled in his coat for a hanky. 'Well, if it is, I'll have her nicked for you. How's that?'

'Sounds good. And make sure you tell the boys to give her a bloody good nudge at the top of a long flight of stairs for me.'

Peter threw his head back and bellowed with laughter. 'We'd soon see if she can fly without her broomstick.'

'Yeah, well, if she doesn't do for me, I reckon he will.'

'What?' Peter wiped his nose again. 'Who you talking about?'

Bill shook his head, instantly regretting letting the words slip out. 'Nothing. Sorry. I was out of order. Nothing.'

'Nothing? Come on. Out with it. What did you mean? Who's "he"?'

'Let's get to the shops, Pete.'

Peter shrugged. 'Go on then, but you know I'm gonna nag you all the way there, all the time we're in Greggs and then all the way back home again.'

Bill looked across at him and sighed.

'Out with it, man.'

Bill started to squirm a bit. 'Cooper.'

'Dr Cooper? Our Dr Cooper? Why? What's he done, then?'

Bill shrugged. 'I don't know. Nothing. Probably nothing.'

'*Probably* nothing? Oh, no. No backtracking! Let's have it.'

Bill turned on the windscreen wipers and watched the first sweep wipe away the rain. 'It's just that . . .'

'What? What is it?' said Peter. 'You're killing me here.'

'It's just that . . . have you ever noticed that people always die a few days after his monthly visit?'

Peter went quiet. 'No. Never thought about it, if I'm honest.'

43

'Well . . . they do.' Bill put the car's transmission into D. 'A bit too often for my liking.'

'Have you mentioned it to anyone?'

'Yeah. Told Charlie. He listened, but I don't think he's taking me seriously.'

'And are you serious, Bill? I mean, that's a big thing to say. You're practically saying he's a murderer.'

'I know. I need to shut up.'

Peter nodded. 'I think it's best, Bill. If the doc ever found out what you're saying he might . . .'

'Might what?'

Peter laughed. 'Might kill you. Oh, God. No. I'm sorry. Shouldn't say that. Got me thinking like you now.'

Bill drove out of the grounds of the home, grinning.

CHAPTER EIGHT

Bill looked up at the clock in the kitchen area: 9 p.m. It was getting late for him, but the lure of two slices of buttered toast and one last cup of tea for the evening had been too much for him to resist. This was also a quiet time. All the other residents would be in their rooms by now, some asleep, some watching the telly, and he would be on his own to enjoy the space that the large kitchen afforded him.

He craned his head over the toaster, taking a minute to enjoy its warmth on his face. The smell of the bread as it cooked wafted into his nostrils. He jumped as the bread popped up and he smiled to himself.

Laying the slices onto the wooden board, he slathered them with butter. Bill wasn't one for this new-fangled 'butter' that filled the shelves of every supermarket he went into. None of this Utterly Butterly or Flora nonsense. He was strictly a half a pound of Anchor man, straight from the fridge. He watched as the knife he was using scraped up little slivers of cold, hard butter and deposited them in some sort of order onto the bread.

He dunked the teabag a couple more times and put his slices of toast on a small plate before wandering off to his favourite seat next to the window.

He was halfway through licking the butter off his fingers from his second slice when Jackie Draper wandered into the kitchen. His heart sank. He said nothing and carried on.

Draper walked over to the kettle. 'This just boiled?' she said, her tone demanding rather than asking.

'Two or three minutes ago,' said Bill.

She tapped her hand on the kettle. 'Shiiit! Why didn't you tell me it was hot?'

Bill searched her face. She hadn't come for tea. 'Mind the kettle. It's hot,' he said.

'What? What'd you say?'

'I said, *Mind the kettle. It's hot.* Don't want you burning yourself.'

Draper picked up the kettle and walked across to Bill's table. He could see she was not happy with his sarcasm. His heart pounded as she quickly crossed the room and stood over him, steam rising from the kettle's spout.

'Think you're funny, old man? Do you?'

Bill's eyes never left the kettle. It crossed his mind she just might pour it over him. 'I'm sorry. I was just joking.'

'Were you? Taking the piss out of me, eh? You think it's funny that I burned myself, eh? Do you?'

'No. No. I'm sorry. I didn't mean anything by it. Please. Put the kettle down. Please.'

Draper fixed her hard stare at Bill, and he felt the heavy weight of her scrutiny as if it were a physical force. His heart skipped a beat, and he shifted uncomfortably in his seat.

She banged the kettle onto the table, and a few little drops of boiling water jumped out of its spout. Bill turned all of his attention to her, feeling suddenly vulnerable in her presence. She looked livid, an angry fire in her eyes, as she dragged out the chair next to him and plonked down her bony frame. She held his gaze for what felt like an eternity, then took a deep breath. 'I want to talk to you, old man.'

Bill licked his lips as his mouth dried. 'What about?'

'What you saw today.'

'Saw?'

'Yeah. You saw me in the office with your little girlfriend, didn't you?'

'Girlfriend? You mean Susan?'

'Oh, got a name, has it?'

'Yes, she has. Susan. As you well know.'

'Yeah, I do know. Smug little stuck-up tart, she is.'

Bill flinched. 'Don't talk about her like that. She's a nice girl.'

'Ah, that's sweet. A nice girl. Do you have little-old-man fantasies running around in your wrinkled old head, eh? Do you imagine her naked, rolling about on your bed? I'll bet you do, you sad old sod.'

Bill's grimaced as he fought to keep out the images Draper had put into his mind. 'Don't be so disgusting. What's wrong with you?'

Draped sat back in her chair. '*I'm* disgusting? I'm not the one pulling my maggoty old peanut under the duvet thinking about her, am I?'

Bill started to pull himself up. 'You're sick, woman.'

'Sit down, pops. I've not finished yet.'

Bill ignored her.

Draper quickly grabbed the kettle and poured some on the floor.

'Shit!' Bill quickly pulled his foot back as a few drops of boiling water splashed his bare ankles and soaked the outside of one slipper.

'Sorry about that,' she said. 'Accident, that was.'

'What do you want?'

'For you to sit back down. That way there won't be any more accidents, will there?'

'That was an accident, was it?'

'I'd have to say yes if I was asked.'

Bill stared into her eyes. There was no way to tell for sure if she would carry out her implied threat but, given that she'd shown willingness to hurt him a few seconds before, it was best not to antagonise her any further. He slowly sat himself back down.

'What?' he said.

'What you saw today . . .'

'You shouting and threatening Susan? Is that what you mean?'

Draper nodded. 'So, you understand, I really don't want to be dragged up in front of another disciplinary. I just want to make sure you're going to keep your gummy old mouth shut. Understand me?'

Bill gave a sharp nod. 'She's a big girl. Nothing to do with me. I didn't see anything, okay. We done?'

A thin-lipped grin spread across Draper's face. 'Just wanted to be sure. You dirty old man, I know how fond you are of her.'

'I told you—'

'I know what you told me, but I've seen you looking at her — a bit too . . . *closely*, shall we say. You really shouldn't look at her like that — you know that, don't you? It'll get you on the sex offenders register and that's not a good look for a cop, is it? Even if you did retire, what, a hundred years ago? What will your mates think of you? Oh, that's right . . . they won't know, will they? They're all bloody dead. And good riddance to the lot of them.'

'You're not a fan of the police, are you, Draper?'

She chuckled. 'You're quick. What'd they used to call you, then? Bullet?'

Bill nodded. 'I'm going back to my room now.'

'Just remember to keep your mouth shut, old man. Or the next accident might be to your hand. Or face. Get me?'

She got up, left the kettle on the table and walked out of the room.

Bill waited until she had left the room before dropping his head into one hand. He wiped his eyes. Tears of anger . . . frustration . . . both.

CHAPTER NINE

Bill pulled back the corner of the worn and slightly stained duvet and sat himself carefully on the bed. He slipped off his dressing gown and left it in a crumpled heap behind his back before wiggling himself along the edge of the bed. He leaned over, picked up the small alarm clock that he'd had for the best part of twenty years and stared at its face. It was late for him: 11.21 p.m. He was normally asleep by now but the altercation with Draper had unsettled him badly.

His hand gently shaking, he put the little clock back on the bedside cabinet. In the dimness cast by the orange light of the lamp beside the clock, he glanced around his humble quarters. A small television sat atop a four-drawer chest. To his left, a two-doored wardrobe held four pairs of trousers, six shirts and three coats: one summer weight, one raincoat and one winter coat. At the bottom were four pairs of shoes: two black, one brown and a pair of trainers. The trainers were the most comfortable and got the most use.

Next to the wardrobe was a sideboard that looked as if it had been built back when genuine craftsmen still made such things. It would last longer than he would.

The carpet was old, grimy and well past its sell-by date, but he wouldn't be getting a replacement any time soon.

Crown Woods Retirement Home was privately run, and although it received a subsidy from the local council, it wasn't enough to make the refurbishments it desperately needed.

He took off his slippers and pushed them under his bed with his heels, just enough to ensure he didn't fall over them on one of his nightly trips to the toilet. He'd fallen over them once before and, as he lay on the floor, couldn't help but see the humour in a once strong, agile man being felled by a pair of sheepskin slippers. To think, after all that he'd seen and done, to be brought down by comfortable footwear. Amid his chuckles, he'd sworn there and then that future Bill wouldn't be killed by a pair of M&S Christmas specials.

Normally, sleep came for him quite quickly, but as he lay there in the dark all he could see was Draper with the kettle in her hand, standing over him.

This world had changed so much for him. There was a time when, although people did bad things, there were rules. Unwritten rules, but rules people didn't transgress. Old people and children . . . they were off-limits, and when someone did hurt them then the full force of the law was brought to bear. If they wound up in prison then God help them. Prisoners had grandparents and kids of their own and never took kindly to new arrivals that had crossed that particular sacred line. It was then that the incarcerated suddenly became all public spirited and would often treat the transgressor with an unexpected trip from the top of a long flight of metal stairs all the way to the bottom with no stops along the way.

There were beatings, stabbings and, dependent on the crime committed, the occasional righteous killing — usually carried out by a lifer with no hope of release.

You don't mess with wrinklies and kiddies. Except times had changed. The newspapers were full of pictures of pensioners being severely beaten for the monthly pittance the government gave them. Conman would enter their homes and steal whatever they could while pretending to be utility workers — or police officers. Children would be snatched from the streets to be spirited away for the pleasure of a pervert or as part of a sex gang. And now care workers threatened old men with boiling kettles.

Bill's eyes were drawn to the top of his wardrobe and the battered old briefcase he kept there. The pull of its contents was too much. He turned on his side and pushed himself up onto one elbow. From there he manoeuvred himself into a seating position before carefully standing up and tottering over to the wardrobe. He reached up and pulled at the case before dragging it off and letting its weight swing his arm down.

He made his way back to his bed and plonked himself down heavily on the mattress before opening the case. Memories. Souvenirs. Obsessions. He reached inside and pulled out torn brown envelopes, document wallets, an old cassette tape and piles of yellowed press cuttings. There was a dogeared paperback book that had seen better days. He pulled it out. His biography. On the front was a picture of a crime scene taken from a stock agency. The title was simple: *Hunting Jack the Knife*.

From his first killing on that layby off the A2, 'Jack' had brought sheer terror to London for the best part of twenty years before disappearing in the year 2005 as suddenly as he had appeared. In those twenty years, Jack had claimed at least thirty-two lives and the police to this day had no real idea of his identity. Whoever Jack was, they were very forensically aware. Everyone involved in the case decided it was a man, due to the level of violence used and the sexual nature of the crimes. Truth be known, nobody knew for certain.

It didn't take the press long to catch on to the fact that the serial killer terrorising London left behind a cassette tape at every murder scene, both sides full of only one track: 'Mack the Knife'. From there it was an easy jump from Mack to Jack and the legend was born. Even today, Bill couldn't listen to the song without feeling his anger rise.

1975 rolled into '76, then '77 and the body count went up and up. William Roach remained as the officer in charge, and the only reason he wasn't removed from the case was because of his sterling record in catching other killers. In his career, Bill had caught and imprisoned twenty-six men and three women for the offence of murder. He was good. Just not good enough to catch Jack.

Every police officer had stories of the 'one that got away', and they would wheel them out at every opportunity: every reunion, every police party, every informal gathering, everyone and anyone who would listen to an old copper still seething at the one who bested them and escaped justice. No copper liked the fact that, for all their knowledge and the resources available to them, someone had somehow managed to stay hidden. And every once in a while, this killer would pop their no-good head out, tear someone to pieces and hide themselves away again. Until the next time.

Even now, in his final years, Bill kept going back over the files, the newspaper cuttings, photocopied statements, everything he had. An image flashed in his head. A girl. In her twenties. Naked. Her face a mask of horror. Fear. Fear of the last face she saw . . . Jack.

Bill shook his head and, for the second time that night, wept for his loss of power.

CHAPTER TEN

Over breakfast, Bill chatted to another resident with whom he'd been friends for the last year. A relatively new arrival, Gary Marks was in his high eighties. A smartly dressed man, Gary had an opinion on just about everything from the state of British sport to how the world should be run and how he would run it if he ever found himself in charge. Charlie nicknamed him 'Know-it-all Gaz'.

Bill and Gary seemed to recognise something in each other, an understanding that needed no further explanation. If they had much life left in front of them, they would probably be lifelong friends. They would often sit together at mealtimes, along with Charlie if he was in the mood. They talked of many things, but each man was loth to probe the others' pasts. It was enough to know that they were cut from similar cloth and, when it came to conversation, that was all that mattered.

Bill, Gary and Charlie were referred to cheekily as the Devil's Triangle by the other residents. It wasn't known who'd started calling them that, but Bill suspected it was probably Lily Keane, a former care worker who'd moved on to other things. She'd had a good sense of humour and was one of the few people who'd made their lives a bit happier.

Bill had just drawn a knife across his fried egg when Gary stiffened suddenly. He dropped the fork he'd been holding and slumped forward, his head making a loud thud as it hit the table.

'Gary?' Charlie shouted. 'Gary!'

'Christ!' said Bill. 'Oh, Christ!'

Bill looked around for Susan, who was the on-duty morning care supervisor. He spotted her at the far end of the dining room, leaning over old Mrs Keller and wiping something off her face. She stopped what she was doing when she heard the thump.

'Susan! Help!' shouted Bill.

She covered the distance from Mrs Keller's table to Bill's in Olympic standard time and tried to rouse Gary. She shook him by the shoulders, calling his name and clicking her fingers by one of his ears. When that drew no response, she pushed him back in his chair. Gary's head wobbled loosely before settling back, chin jutting forward into the air.

'Bill?' she said, a hint of desperation in her voice.

Bill lifted himself from his chair. 'Get him on the floor. Lay him on his back. Mind his head.'

By the time Bill had got up, Susan had done exactly what he'd told her. Bill recognised the greyish colour that had replaced Gary's normally reddish complexion. It didn't take a doctor to realise that. Gary was in the middle of a heart attack. 'Get an ambulance!' he snapped.

'But . . .' Susan seemed unsure. Though she'd had some first aid training, she looked as though her limbs were refusing to cooperate with her brain.

'Go, Susan!' Bill lowered himself carefully to his knees, cursing silently. Getting back up was going to be a whole new crisis for him. Susan ran, leaving Bill and Charlie to administer first aid.

By the time an ambulance arrived, Bill had restarted his friend's heart and had made him as comfortable as he could. It pleased him that there was at least a little bit of colour back in Gary's cheeks. Charlie had grabbed the cushion that old Mrs Park sat on and placed it under Gary's head. Mrs Dunbar had run out of her office with a thick woollen blanket that she used to cover Gary. It was left to Susan and Charlie to help Bill back to his feet, and he moaned and groaned every inch of the way. Men of his age were not supposed to be down on the floor giving first aid.

As Gary was loaded onto a stretcher, one paramedic thanked Bill for his help and went to pains to point out that his actions had probably saved his friend.

'Which hospital are you taking him to?' said Susan.

'St Bart's,' said the paramedic. 'You coming with him?'

Susan turned to Mrs Dunbar. She nodded.

'Let me grab my coat and I'll be with you,' she said.

'No mad rush, love. We'll be a few minutes ourselves.'

Loaded and strapped onto the stretcher, the paramedics walked out of the building toward the waiting ambulance.

Susan, coat in hand, called to Mrs Dunbar. 'I'll call as soon as I know what's going on.'

CHAPTER ELEVEN

Bill grabbed onto the handrail at the entrance to St Bartholomew's Hospital, a mix of weathered bricks and tall glass windows. He paused for a moment to take in the sight of this distinguished medical institution that had even made it into the world of fiction. Sir Arthur Conan Doyle's 1887 novel, *A Study in Scarlet*, began with a meeting between the greatest detective who never lived, Sherlock Holmes, and his sidekick, Dr Watson, in a chemical laboratory at Bart's.

St Bartholomew's Hospital was Britain's oldest working hospital, and had been around for 900 years, still offering medical services in its original spot. It was known around the world as a symbol of excellence in cancer and heart care, so Gary was in very good hands.

With each step, Bill's thoughts turned to his age and all the ailments that came with it. He was no fan of hospitals but, as he got older, it seemed that he visited them more and more often. At least today, he was just a visitor and not a patient.

Once inside the main hospital entrance, he had a quick discussion with a volunteer who pointed him toward Gary's ward. Bill thanked her, took a conveniently placed seat outside a small cafeteria and waited for Charlie.

He looked around him and couldn't help but notice how much hospitals had changed since he was a kid. Where the walls were either a dirty cream colour with a battleship-grey bottom half, now they were painted a brilliant white, marked by grubby hands and a general lack of cleanliness. Small windows had been replaced with large, double-glazed units that allowed him to see into a small community garden and the odd ward. Gone was the stink of a disinfectant so strong it penetrated the throat and burrowed deep into the memory.

There were no more matrons, women who ran the wards with a rod of iron. If anyone dared to transgress any rule on the matron's ward, they would come to regret it. It was the matron who ensured that the ward was spotlessly clean and remained so. Two visitors were allowed per patient and that was it. If one was a child visiting a sick parent, they were expected to sit on a chair and not climb on the bed. And they had better not. He'd long held the belief that the lack of disinfectant and matrons had contributed to the rise of people catching other diseases in hospital.

The arrival of a smiling Charlie brought him out of his thoughts.

'You get parked alright?' Bill said.

'Yep. It's busy but I managed to squeeze in on a corner. You seen the price of parking? Jesus! It's not pensioner friendly.'

'I know. Robbery.' Bill started to stand up. The volunteer watched him rise, a look of concern on her face as he struggled to pull himself upright. Charlie took his arm and steadied him.

'You found out where he is?'

'Yeah. He's in the Cardiac Department.'

'Do you need a wheelchair?'

Bill looked at him and shook his head. 'I can walk, thank you.'

'Can you, though? You're not too clever on the old legs these days, Bill.'

Charlie turned to the volunteer. 'Excuse me . . . My friend here's a bit dodgy on his legs. D'you think he'll need a wheelchair to get to the . . .'

'Cardiac?' said the volunteer. 'It might be a bit of a walk for him. I'll get you a wheelchair if you like?'

'I'm right here!' snarled Bill. 'And I'm fine! I can make it. It just might take a little while.'

Charlie looked at his watch. 'Well, it's four o'clock now and this place shuts at eight, so I dunno if we'll make it in time, you doddery old sod. Yes please, love. A wheelchair would be helpful.'

'I don't want a wheelchair, Charlie. I can walk. I've got my stick.'

'And I can't afford fourteen hours' worth of parking while you dodder about. So, wheelchair it is.'

Bill sighed. There was little point in arguing. 'Fine, I'll take it,' he said to the volunteer. 'Thank you.'

CHAPTER TWELVE

A soon as Charlie pushed Bill out of the lift, Bill told him he wanted out of the chair.

'What? Why?' said Charlie. 'Just stay in it and let me keep pushing you,' said Charlie.

'I don't want him to see me in a wheelchair, that's why.'

'Why not? It's not like he's going to take too much notice of you, is it? He's had a bloody heart attack.'

'Not the point. If I go in there, I go in under my own steam.'

Charlie shrugged. 'Okay . . . alright, suit yerself.' He put the brake on the wheelchair and held it steady as Bill hauled himself up and out of it. As he doddered his way down the short hallway to the nurses' desk, Bill spotted Gary and stopped. He was lying in a propped-up position, wires attached to his bony chest and an oxygen mask covering his nose and mouth. He shook his head and waited for Charlie, who had gone to report their arrival to the receptionist.

Charlie told her who they were there to see and, after a quick conversation with her, made his way back to Bill. They walked in and took up position either side of Gary's bed. Though drugged up, Gary was still able to open his eyes slowly. He gave them both a faint smile.

'How you doing, boys?' The words slurred against each other as he fought against the medication.

'Yeah, we're all right, Gary,' said Bill.

'Better than you, that's for sure,' said Charlie.

Gary managed a smile. 'True. True.'

'Nurse said that it's not so bad,' said Charlie. 'A small blockage in your pipes. They'll fix you up, dose you up and you'll be out of here before you know it.'

'Good to know.' Gary grimaced as he tried to move. 'Got a feeling it might be a bit longer than *before I know it*, though.'

'Maybe. But the important thing is that you get well.'

'Yeah, c'mon, Gary,' Bill said. 'I miss my old mate. Charlie's not as sophisticated as you.'

Charlie's eyes widened. 'Not sophisticated? Me? Piss off, you old fart.'

Bill shook his head. 'See what I mean?'

The little group had a chuckle between themselves until Gary started coughing.

'You alright?' said Bill.

'Yeah. I'm okay.' Gary held up a hand. 'Seriously . . . don't worry.'

After an uncomfortable minute of Gary coughing, he settled back down and gave his friends a weak smile.

'Are they testing for anything else, Gary?' said Bill.

'Like what?' said Charlie. 'He's had a tiny heart attack.'

'I know. I was just asking.'

Charlie frowned at him.

'Have the doctors said what will happen to you when you come out?'

Gary shook his head. 'No. Nothing yet. Why?'

Bill shrugged. 'No reason. Just asking.'

Charlie shook his head. 'Not this again, Bill.'

'What?'

'You know what. You're going to swing this around to Dr Cooper again, aren't you?'

'No, I was just asking. Making conversation.'

'Were you?'

'Yes.'

'Hmm. You've got to get this idea out of your head, Bill. It's bloody ridiculous.'

'What idea?' said Gary. 'What are you talking about?'

'It's nothing. Some crackpot idea the ex-copper's got into his head.'

'What? What is it?'

Charlie shook his head. 'Tell him,' he said to Bill. 'That should cheer him up no end.'

Bill looked across to his friend. Charlie should have kept his mouth shut.

'It's just that I've noticed . . . I've noticed that whenever the doc's been to the home to do his rounds, someone dies a couple of days later. It just strikes me as odd, that's all.'

Gary nodded. 'Yeah, me too.'

Bill's face lit up. 'You've noticed it?'

'Mm-hm.'

'Why didn't you say anything?'

'Who to? Mrs Dunbar? What will she say? An old person died in their sleep. And?'

'Yeah, but what about the police?'

'Your mob? No mate. It's the same thing, isn't it? I can hear it now. "Hello officer. Something rather peculiar's happened. I'd like to report a dead person in an old people's home." I'm sure they'd all come charging round for that.'

Charlie smiled. 'That what I keep telling him.'

'I'm not saying it's not a bit strange though,' said Gary. 'Wouldn't surprise me if he is bumping people off.'

Charlie snorted. 'Now you're getting like Bill. Why would Cooper want to knock off us old wrinklies? For the money? That wouldn't work, would it? The families would be onto that like a bolt of lightning. I doubt he gets his jollies off by it, so why would he do it?'

'Because he can.' Bill's voice was flat and calm. 'God complex. Lot of doctors have it.'

'Like a lot of old people have stupid ideas. More so, paranoid old coppers. You're just being silly, Bill. Let it go.'

Bill shook his head. 'No. The old alarms are going off. I know he's up to something. I can feel it. It's a warm sensation.'

'Ain't pissed yourself have you?'

Gary's chuckle turned into a cough and his two friends watched as his face turned red.

'Easy, Gary,' said Bill. 'Easy.'

Gary held up his hand again and left it there until he'd regained his composure.

'I think he needs a rest.' A young nurse standing behind the friends didn't look impressed. 'I need to check his vitals now and his dinner will be around soon. So, if you gentlemen don't mind . . .' She held her hand out toward the exit.

'But we've only just got here, love,' Charlie protested.

'I'm sorry. But there's things to do. Come back tomorrow — perhaps a bit earlier.'

'Seriously?'

'Seriously,' said the nurse.

Charlie sighed. 'Come on then, old timer,' he said to Bill. 'Time to go. Gary, see you soon.'

Bill patted his friend's hand and said his goodbyes. 'I'll try and come back tomorrow, mate.'

'Don't worry, Bill. I won't be here too long. I can't wait to get back to see that lovely, caring old cow, Draper.' The two men had a little chuckle before the stern look on the nurse's face broke them up.

Once outside the ward, Bill reluctantly got back in the wheelchair and the two men headed off toward the exit.

'That was a bloody waste of time,' said Charlie. 'Miserable little mare, that nurse was.'

'Probably busy and a bit stressed. Tough old game being a nurse. We're lucky to have them.'

'Yeah, I know that but, Jesus, we were only in there, what, five minutes? She could have shown us a bit of the old compassion they're all famous for.'

Bill chuckled. 'So. What d'you think, then?'

'About what?'

'About what Gary said. He agrees with me about Cooper.'

62

'Bill, this is becoming an obsession. You either do something about it, or you let it go.'

'I know, I know. I just can't get it out of my head.'

'Look . . . if you're serious, report it to the police officially. You know that. It's all you can do.'

'Gary's spotted the pattern.'

'Gary's off his tits on drugs. He don't know what he's saying.'

The two men remained silent all the way to the lift and stayed that way until Charlie wheeled Bill into it.

'Charlie . . .'

Charlie pressed the button for the ground floor. 'What?'

'I'm going to do it.'

'Oh yeah? Do what?'

'I'm going to expose him.'

CHAPTER THIRTEEN

Susan Johnson watched Bill and Charlie faffing about at the entrance to Crown Woods on the office security camera as they made their way in through the main doors and along the short corridor to the reception desk.

Getting his balance, Bill lifted his walking stick slightly in greeting.

'Hi, Bill. Hi, Charlie. How are you two?'

'All good, love,' said Bill. 'Just been to see old Gary.'

'And?'

'He's doing all right, I suppose. Looks a bit grey and coughing a lot. Don't know where he got that from.'

Susan averted her gaze for a second and fumbled in her pocket before looking back at him. 'He's had that cough for a long time, you know that.'

Bill shrugged. 'Yeah. Thinking about it, he has, hasn't he? Just seemed worse, that's all.'

'When are they letting him out? Have they said?'

'Nope,' said Charlie. 'Probably keep him in a for a day or two at the most, then they'll boot him out. They need the beds, don't they?'

Susan nodded. 'Well, as long as he's fit enough when they do let him out or I'll be up there after them.'

Both of the old men smiled.

'You can come up after me, if you like,' said Charlie with cheeky grin on his face.

'Charlie! Don't be rude,' said Bill.

'She's all right. She's a big girl. She knows I'm only playing.'

'Praying more like,' said Susan. 'I'd kill you, old man.'

Charlie grinned. 'I'd be very happy to let you kill me. I wouldn't mind that on me death certificate . . . killed by a beautiful young blonde while having a bit of nookie. That's pride, that is.'

Susan giggled. 'Nookie? What the hell is nookie? I've never heard it called that.'

'Nookie?' said Charlie. 'Nookie's a bit of . . . y'know, a bit of the old how's yer father.'

'What? What's *that*?'

'Christ! Don't you kids know anything these days? It's the same thing. Y'know . . .'

Susan shook her head. 'What?'

'Sex,' Charlie whispered. 'It means *sex*.'

'Does it? I've never heard it called that before.'

'That's because you've never stepped out with anyone fifty-odd years older than yourself,' said Bill.

'Not you and all, Bill. *Stepped out?* That's a really old saying.'

'Have you not seen us?' he said with a chuckle. 'We're old!'

'C'mon, you two old reprobates. Hang your coats up and I'll make you both a cuppa. What'd you want in yours, Charlie? Viagra?'

'It'll take more than a little blue tablet to help me out, love. I'd need a tiny little splint!'

Susan laughed as she waltzed off toward the kitchen. 'I'll just put in two sugars. Same as usual.'

* * *

Charlie hung his coat up then helped Bill, who was struggling with his. 'Bill, let go of your stick.'

'What?'

'Your stick. Stand it against the wall. Then you'll have two hands free, won't you, you silly old sod?'

'All right, all right. I know.'

'Well, why didn't you do it?' Charlie tugged at Bill's sleeve until his arm came free.

'I didn't think.'

'That's because you can't. Your brain's gone, you silly old sod.'

'Don't keep calling me that.'

'Sorry . . . sorry. Here y'are. Gimme your coat.' Charlie hung Bill's coat up and muttered something under his breath that sounded suspiciously like 'Silly old sod.'

'What? You say something?'

'I said, I'm looking forward to me tea.'

'Hmm.' Bill wandered off in the direction of the kitchen.

'Bill!' Charlie called.

Bill stopped and turned. Charlie was standing there holding up Bill's walking stick. 'Don't forget yer stick, yer silly old sod.'

'Fair enough,' said Bill, as he snatched the stick from Charlie.

CHAPTER FOURTEEN

Bill, Charlie and Susan had been sitting around the table drinking tea and dunking biscuits for ten minutes or so when Mrs Dunbar approached them.

Susan started, as if expecting a rebuke, although she knew Mrs Dunbar wasn't really one for that sort of thing. Mrs Dunbar held up her hand to Susan. 'I just wanted to tell you all something.'

Bill frowned.

'What's up?' said Charlie. 'Is it good news? Has old misery guts Draper had an accident? Is she hurt? Is it bad? Is she dead? Can we have a party?'

Bill and Susan both chuckled. Mrs Dunbar looked shocked.

'What? No. What a terrible thing to say, Charlie.'

'Is it?' he said. 'It's not like anyone'd miss her, would they? I mean, c'mon. She's an awful woman.'

'That's still an awful thing to say, Charlie, and you know it.'

'Do I, though? Would you miss her?'

'She's a valuable member of st—'

'She's a wicked cow!' Bill spat the words out with venom.

'Bill! Don't you join in. He's bad enough with the terrible things he says. I don't need you joining in.'

'Truth's truth, Mrs D,' he said.

Susan looked down at her feet, trying not to laugh at Mrs Dunbar's indignation.

'Okay,' said Bill. 'Sorry. What did you want to tell us?'

Mrs Dunbar patted herself down and cleared her throat. 'It's about your friend, Gary.'

The table went silent.

'This won't come as a shock to you, Susan, but I've just had a call from Bart's, the ward where Gary is staying. One of the doctors there tells me they've carried out x-rays and scans and it seems his pulmonary disease is much further advanced than they first thought.'

'What?' said Bill. 'Pulmonary disease? He went in for his heart. I didn't know he had that.'

Charlie shook his head. 'Me neither. How long's he had that?'

'Couple of years. He didn't want anyone to know. Not even you two.'

Bill looked across at Susan. 'Did you know this?'

She nodded but kept from meeting his eyes.

'Of course she knew, Bill,' said Mrs Dunbar. 'She's a carer. Thing is, they say he's now entering the terminal stage. I'm sorry.'

The others froze at the word *terminal*.

'Terminal? What d'you mean, terminal?' Bill felt his bottom lip begin to tremble.

Mrs Dunbar shuffled her feet awkwardly but Charlie saved her the embarrassment. 'How long does he have?'

She shrugged. 'I don't know. The hospital's reluctant to give out time frames. Everyone's different, of course. Could be weeks, could be months. I doubt he'll last more than a few months, though.'

Bill pulled his shoulders back. 'Oh, Jesus. He's such a good man. He doesn't deserve this.'

Charlie shook his head and rubbed a hand over his face. 'Doesn't matter what he deserves, Bill. If it did, every murderer in the world would be dead.'

'When are they letting him out?' Susan asked.

'Soon. Maybe tomorrow,' said Mrs Dunbar. 'His heart attack was minor, by all accounts. It just took him badly because of the other thing. All went a bit wrong for him.'

'Tomorrow?' said Bill.

'There y'are,' said Charlie. 'Told you they'd boot him as soon as. Useless sods!'

Mrs Dunbar scowled at him. 'No need for that language, Charlie.'

Charlie scowled back at her. 'That's not what I really wanted to say, believe me.'

'What time tomorrow?' said Bill.

'I'm not sure it will be tomorrow,' said Mrs Dunbar. 'I have to ring to find out. But if it is, they tell me it won't be until late afternoon. Then they have to get his meds and stuff. They said they'd let us know when he was ready for collection.'

Bill nodded. 'Then what? When he gets here?'

Mrs Dunbar sighed. 'Well, he'll be released with some paperwork that I have to check, and Dr Cooper will have to come to make sure that he really doesn't need to be in hospital and then he'll keep an eye on him.'

Bill snorted. 'I'd say he has a lot less than a couple of months, then.'

All heads turned toward him.

'I'm sorry?' said Mrs Dunbar. 'What does that mean?'

Bill saw Charlie shaking his head and making a cut-throat sign behind Mrs Dunbar's back.

'You know what it means.'

'Bill . . . *No.*' Charlie's tone was serious enough for Bill to acknowledge him.

'What?' said Bill. 'You mark my words.'

'What's he talking about?' said Mrs Dunbar. 'What's he mean?'

'What I mean, Mrs Dunbar, is that I've noticed that every time Dr Cooper examines someone, they tend to die within a day or two.'

Mrs Dunbar's jaw dropped open slightly. 'Bill! Don't be so ridiculous. That's a terrible thing to say. Dr Cooper is a fine doctor and we're lucky to have him.'

'Tell that to his last three victims.'

'That's enough, Bill,' said Susan. 'That sort of talk will get you into a lot of trouble.'

Bill shrugged. 'Check your records, Mrs Dunbar. See if I'm right.'

Mrs Dunbar rose from her chair. 'I'm not listening to this nonsense. Bill, I think you're in shock, that's why you're saying these things. Susan, please make him another cup of tea — with a lot more sugar in it this time. I'm going back to my office.' With that, she turned on her heel and strode off.

'Bill,' said Charlie. 'You need to be careful, mate. That's slander, that is. It's alright sounding off to me or Susan, but you can't go saying that to her. Not like that. Like I said, report your concerns officially. Don't just chuck it out there over a cuppa.'

'Slander? What's he gonna do? Sue me? Good luck with that. What are they gonna take from me? I don't have a pot to piss in.'

Charlie got up from the table. 'I'm off to watch the telly. Susan, keep an eye on Sherlock Bloody Holmes here. G'night.'

'G'night,' said Susan. She made her way over to the counter and flicked the kettle switch. 'Three sugars, Bill?'

Bill felt a single tear snake its way down his cheek. He sniffled and, in an attempt to keep his composure, dabbed at the snot that dangled off his nose before turning away. 'I have to stop him, Susan. You must see that.'

Susan sighed and gazed at him fondly. 'I think we'll make it four sugars.'

CHAPTER FIFTEEN

Bill looked at the clock over the door of the little cafeteria where he and Charlie sat. He put down his cup of tea on the saucer, careful not to spill any. 'How much longer are we going to have to wait?'

Charlie shrugged. 'Dunno, pal. Hopefully, not too much longer.'

'You said that half an hour after we got here. We've been, what, three hours?'

'Three hours and nine minutes.'

'*Three hours and nine minutes?* No wonder this country's in such a bloody state.'

Charlie scrunched his face up. 'What's a three hour wait got to do with the state of the country?'

'Everything. It's typical of the fact that nobody cares anymore.'

'They care, Bill. They're just busy. It's how it is now. Just relax. Drink yer tea and suck yer digestive. He'll be ready soon.'

'Ten more minutes then I'm going in and getting loud.'

Charlie smiled. 'I'm looking forward to that. You're as quiet as a church mouse at the best of times, so this should be good!'

Charlie's mobile phone rang. He answered it, nodded two or three times, said, 'Thank you very much,' and hung up. 'Here we go, mate. He's ready for us.' Charlie kicked off the brake on Bill's wheelchair and the two set off to collect their friend.

After another wait of thirty minutes in which more forms got signed, the trio finally got underway. A porter wheeled Gary out. The three friends said very little other than to greet Gary and ask how he was feeling. After that, it was silence all the way to the car.

Once the porter had gone, they felt more able to talk.

'It's bloody good to see you, mate,' said Bill.

Gary nodded. 'Thanks.'

'Thought they'd changed their minds and decided to keep you in there, the amount of time they took,' said Charlie.

'I know,' said Gary. He opened the door and carefully sat himself down in the rear passenger seat while Charlie helped Bill into the front. Slowly and carefully, Bill pulled his legs in and then wiggled around until he was comfortable.

'Belts on, ladies,' said Charlie. He started the engine and waited another two minutes as his friends struggled with finding the buckles on their seats.

'Let me help you, Bill,' he said, patience exhausted.

'I can do it. Give me a minute. Where is it?'

'Down the side where it always is. Let me do it.'

'I said I can do it.' Bill fiddled around until he heard a satisfying click. 'Got it.'

'Thank the Lord,' said Charlie as he pulled out of his parking space.

'How d'you feel, Gary?' said Bill.

'Tired, if I'm honest.' He yawned loudly as if to emphasise the point.

'You can have a nice kip when we get back. Do you good. Can't believe they let you out so soon.'

Gary chuckled. 'I know. Bloody liberty, it is.'

'I'm glad there was nothing really wrong with your heart, Gary,' said Charlie. 'Had us all worried, you did,'

'Yeah, sorry about that, fellahs. Bit of a surprise to me as well.'

'I'll bet. Still, might have been a better ending for you.'

Bill jerked his head right to glare at Charlie.

'What d'you mean?' said Gary.

'Your lung disease,' said Charlie. 'We know about it.'

'Christ, Charlie,' said Bill. 'That's out of order.'

Gary dropped his shoulders and looked out of the car window.

'Were you going to tell us, your old mates, at any point?' said Charlie.

'Wasn't the plan. I didn't want to worry you. You know how it is.'

Charlie nodded. He slowed the car down as he approached a red light, then sped up as it turned green. 'I do know. Thing is, that's the sort of thing you share with friends.'

'Why? What can you do about it? It is what it is.'

'You're right. It is what it is. But we could have helped you more. Spent a bit more time with you. Took you out shopping a bit more if you needed it. That sort of thing, y'know?'

'Sounds like sympathy to me,' said Len.

Charlie shrugged. 'What's wrong with a bit of that?'

'It's not for me. Look, I know you boys mean well but I'm not looking for sympathy. We've all got our own problems, haven't we? You've got a problem with your kidneys and veins, and Bill's got his diabetes and that other thing — Anderson's, is it?'

'Addison's,' said Bill.

'That's it. So, I'm not complaining and I'm not after sympathy.'

'Okay, fair enough,' said Charlie. 'I'm sorry. Didn't mean to upset you.'

'You haven't upset me, mate. Sorry if I sounded harsh. I'm just not one for fuss.'

'Gary,' said Bill. 'I hear you have to see Dr Cooper tomorrow for some follow-up checks. You okay with that?'

'Yeah, I know.'

'You don't have to have him, you know. You can ask for another doctor to see you.'

'I know I can. You think I should?'

'Well . . . y'know . . .'

'What?'

'He thinks the doc is killing off the residents,' Charlie said. 'He's drivin' me mad with it.'

'What?' said Gary.

'To be fair,' said Bill. 'You agreed with me.'

'Did I?' said Gary.

'Yeah. Spoke about it when we came to see you.'

'That was you two, was it? I thought two of God's little helpers had visited me. I must've been off my head with the drugs, Bill. Sorry.'

Bill's shoulders sank. Gary wasn't the ally he wanted. 'Just be careful, Gary, that's all I'm saying. Watch what he gives you.'

Gary sighed. 'Yeah, okay. Thanks for your concern, mate. Appreciated. I'm gonna have a little doze back here for ten minutes, if you don't mind. I'm knackered.'

Bill could tell from Gary's tone that his input wasn't appreciated at all.

CHAPTER SIXTEEN

When the trio got back to the home, they took themselves off to their respective rooms. Bill was in the only comfortable chair in his room, a large high-backed effort with wings that encircled his head. It was too heavy to move around without help and so he had it positioned right where it would stay for the rest of his life. Just enough light for him during the morning to read his newspaper and dull enough in the afternoon for him to nod off to sleep without the harsh glare of sunlight on his face. He got little sun in his room, but he was okay with that — never was much of a sun bunny.

Settled now, he began to nod off, tired after the day's events. With one hand resting on his cheek and his legs outstretched, his breathing gradually changed and slowed right down.

Then he jerked out of his dozing fit as he felt his heart leap in fright.

Draper had barged in, shoving the door wide open and announcing herself in her loud, bellowing voice. 'Right! Time for a clear-up!'

'What the fu—'

'Let's go, old man! C'mon! Chop, chop! This place is a bloody pigsty, it is.'

'Get out, you bitch! Leave me alone!'

She looked at him with contempt and a hint of anger. 'Bitch, am I?'

'Yes, you are. Now get out!'

She chuckled. 'When I've had a tidy up. Until then, go downstairs and get a cup of tea or something.'

Bill felt the colour rise to his face and his heart was thumping as Draper swiftly snatched Bill's items from the dressing table, throwing them into an oversized plastic bag.

'What are you doing?' Bill lunged forward. 'That's my stuff! My—'

'Rubbish,' Draper spat. She dropped the bag and, as he scrambled through it to reclaim his stuff, she took advantage of his moment of distraction to leap up and grab his suitcase from the top of the wardrobe before he could stop her.

He looked up at the sound the case made as it scraped against the wood. 'What? No! Leave it! Leave it! That's private!' The bin bag forgotten, he turned all of his attention toward the suitcase. He lunged forward, only to be blocked by Draper's bony frame and, as hard he tried to get past her, she blocked him all the way. 'Don't you touch that! Leave it alone!'

'What's in it, old man? Your collection of dirty mags, hmm? Big collection, is it? Feels heavy.' She leaned forward and clicked open one of the latches. This fired Bill up even more. He shoved her to one side and made a grab for the case.

'Hey, hey, hey!' She was angry now. 'What're you worried about? Secrets, eh?'

Bill saw an opening and made another grab for the case. This time, he grabbed the handle and snatched it away. Draper wasn't giving up her prize easily, though. She grabbed the case by the edges and the two of them got into a push–pull battle. It must have surprised Draper just how strong Bill was in his desperation to wrest his case out of her hands. The two of them shouted at each other until something finally gave out. In this case, it was Draper, who hadn't quite got a good enough grip of the edges. As she let go, Bill fell backward onto the sideboard and hit the case against its edge. The remaining closed latch gave up the fight and the case burst open, sending it contents spilling out onto the floor.

'You cow! Look what you've done. My stuff! My stuff!'

He got down onto his knees fast. Draper looked surprised at this sudden burst of agility, even under these circumstances. As Bill scrabbled to get the fallen paperwork back into the case, Draper swooped down and swifted away the paperback book. He reached up with a bony hand but she was too quick. She hid it behind her back before stepping away and looking at its cover. '*Hunting Jack the Knife.*'

He grabbed at it but she turned away.

'What's it say? *The one who got away. DCI William Roach.*' She flicked through the book but seemed disinterested in the pages. 'That you, is it, old man? You this DCI Roach then, are you? And who's this Jack the Knife, then? Oh, wait a minute. I remember. Wasn't he the one who killed all them women back in the eighties and nineties? Yeah. Yeah, it was. So, you were in charge of the investigation, were you?'

'Give it back!' Bill demanded.

'No wonder he got away,' she snorted. 'Surely they had someone better than you to chase after him.'

Bill pulled himself to his feet and made a snatch for the book.

'Ah-ah.' Draper moved away again. She began to read the back cover out loud. '*This is the story of one of Britain's most notorious serial killers, known only to the police as "Jack the Knife", and the detective who dedicated his life to bringing him to justice.*'

She shook her head at him. 'Waste of your life, then, wasn't it? Never did catch him, did you?' A light went on in her head. 'Wait a minute. What if it was you all along? What if you were the killer? That's why he never got caught. You covered it all up, you crafty old sod. Yeah, yeah. That's it. It's you.'

Bill shook his head, his heart filled with rage at this woman's torment of him. 'Don't be so damned insulting. I spent my bloody career chasing—'

'Yeah, I know. It says.' She tossed the book at him and he grabbed at it as if it was the most precious thing in the world. Safely in his hands, he clutched it to his chest, like a bible.

'Get out!' he yelled at her. 'Just get out!'

'What's going on in here?' Mrs Dunbar stood in the doorway of Bill's room. Susan stood just off to the side. 'What are you doing here, Mrs Draper?' she demanded.

'Nothing. Just helping Bill to tidy up his room. He asked me to earlier.'

Mrs Dunbar glanced at Bill. She could see from his demeanour that he was visibly upset and that the floor was strewn with papers. 'Is that so? I heard shouting. What was that about?'

Draper shrugged. 'I grabbed his old suitcase off the top of the wardrobe and he freaked out. Dunno why.'

'Bill. Is that what happened?'

Draper glared at Bill.

Bill glared back. 'No. This cow came in here to cause me trouble. She broke my suitcase and emptied out the papers on the floor. Picked up my book and started taking the piss out of me.'

Draper looked taken aback. 'What? That's absolutely *not* what happened.'

Susan poked her head around the door frame and gave Bill a reassuring smile. He perked up on seeing her.

'Oh, what's she doing here?' asked Draper.

'I asked her to come with me. I heard the shouting. I think it high time you left this room, Mrs Draper. Go downstairs and wait in my office.'

'What?'

'You heard. My office. We need to talk about this little incident.'

Draper shook her head and gave a little smile. 'Yes, boss. Whatever you say.' With that, she barrelled her way over the door, forcing Mrs Dunbar to one side, and swaggered off down the hallway — but not before turning to Susan and mouthing the word *bitch* at her.

Both Mrs Dunbar and Susan helped Bill to recover his paperwork and put it all back into his suitcase.

'There you go, Bill,' said Mrs Dunbar. 'All back now. I'm sorry about her behaviour.'

Bill shook his head. 'She's an awful woman, Mrs Dunbar. Can't you just sack her? We'd all be better off.'

She gave Bill a kind smile, the sort she gave to all the old residents when they asked her something she couldn't deliver. 'It's not that easy, Bill. I just can't get the cover these days. It's so difficult.'

Bill nodded. 'Can you keep her away from me, then? She's going out of her way to make me miserable, it seems, and I don't know why. I never did anything to her.'

'I'll see what I can do. I can't promise, mind, but I'll see.'

'Thank you,' said Bill. 'I'd appreciate that.'

'Susan, can you stay with Bill for a while. Make sure he's settled again and keep an eye on him, eh?'

'Of course I will. Happy to.'

Mrs Dunbar stepped out of the room and headed for her showdown with Draper.

Susan gave Bill a smile. 'You okay?'

'Mm-hm.'

'Really?'

'Really.'

'Good.' She pointed at the suitcase. 'Now, you crafty old devil . . . we need to talk about all of this, don't we?'

CHAPTER SEVENTEEN

Susan settled Bill into his chair and draped a thin woollen blanket over his legs. Bill cuffed his nose on the back of his sleeve and looked at Susan.

'What is it you want to know?' he said.

Susan picked up the paperback bearing his name. 'Well, this for starters. You never told me you were a famous detective.'

Bill waved his hand at her. 'Famous? I'm not famous. Not at all.'

'But you've written a book.'

'I didn't. It's a biography. Someone else did. Doesn't make me famous, Susan. Not at all.'

She flicked through the pages. 'Okay, but this was a very important case, wasn't it? And you were the one in charge, were you?'

He nodded. 'Mm-hm. Didn't catch him, though. Scumbag got away from me. The only one who did.'

'What? I thought you said you caught everybody you went after.'

Bill dropped his gaze for a second. 'Well, yeah. *Nearly* a hundred per cent clear-up rate. But this is the one that people always remember me for. The one that got away. They say that every detective has a case that haunts them, and this one is mine. I just don't talk about it because he out-thought me at every turn. I just wasn't clever enough for him.'

Susan nodded. 'Yeah, I understand. But you did your best, didn't you? I know you'll have done your best. It's who you are, Bill. You're a good man.'

He smiled at her. 'Yeah, maybe. Just not good enough, eh?'

She dug into the papers she'd dropped into the suitcase and rummaged around before pulling out a brown cardboard docket. 'Are these . . .'

'Case papers?' said Bill. 'Yes. Well, copies, not the originals. They're stored away.'

'Are you supposed to have these?'

Bill shrugged. 'Nope. But I've got 'em. The thing about the ones that get away is that they really never *go* away. Not for the ones chasing them. I kept these, copies of every last bit of paper connected to the case, so that I could keep going over them. Keep looking for the one bit of evidence or clue that I must have missed. I must have.'

Susan frowned at him and went back to the suitcase. She pulled another envelope out of the pile, brown A4.

'Ah-ah,' said Bill. 'Don't think you'll want to look in there, love. Crime scene photos. They're really not nice.'

She hesitated, a grimace on her face. 'No?'

'No. But, it's your choice. You're a big girl and, well, if you want to get in with the police, you're going to see some bloody awful things. Up to you.' He gave her a weak grin.

Susan hesitated, then went for it. She pulled out the pile of photographs and her eyes widened as she looked at the first one. 'My God!'

Bill craned his neck to see who she was looking at. 'Carrie Reece. Murdered on her twenty-second birthday. Coming home from some drinks with her work colleagues when she was attacked from behind. Killer put his hand over her mouth and rammed a carving knife up and under her ribcage. Straight in the heart. She was dead within a few minutes but, before she died, he cut her nose off. She got off lightly.'

Susan's hand was over her mouth. 'Oh, dear God! Poor girl!'

Bill nodded. 'Yep. Wrong place, wrong time.'

She looked at another one before showing it to Bill. 'Hmm. That's Linda Hall. She was twenty-four. He caught her crossing a field late at night. She was a bit tipsy and not walking, or thinking, straight. Decided to take a shortcut home. Never made it. He killed her within a few hundred yards of the home she shared with her boyfriend. He slashed her throat and, while she lay dying, he ripped open her blouse and . . . C'mere, give me the envelope.' Susan handed it to him. He flicked through a few photos, pulled one out and handed it to her. 'Cut her breasts off. We found one of them caught in a bush. Think a dog had the other.'

Susan looked sideways at him. 'Jesus, Bill. How can you be so . . .'

'What? Matter-of-fact?'

'Don't these upset you?'

'No. Not anymore. Not like they used to. I've seen them so many times, and the fact is coppers are hardened to this sort of thing. Have to be. If they weren't, the job wouldn't get done, would it? Same for ambulance men . . . fire brigade . . . soldiers . . . They all see crappy things and they all get dealt with. That's it.'

'How many did he kill? Do you know?'

'Thirty-two that we know about, that we can definitely say was down to him, but in total? Probably same again. Probably more. Just can't be definite on them.'

'My God, Bill. I had no idea.'

'Of what?'

'Of what you did. I mean, I knew you were a CID man, but I thought it was all pen pushing and meetings.'

Bill chuckled. 'Well, sometimes it is. Got my hands dirty a lot of the time and saw way too many things that I can't forget. Y'never know, maybe the dementia will take me a bit sooner. That'd be nice.'

'Don't say that, Bill. That's terrible.'

'Is it? Might give me some peace of mind. There are some memories I could do with losing, love.'

Susan looked back into the suitcase. 'Did you have any idea of who he was?'

He shrugged. 'Initially, we had suspects. Suspects by the bucketload. A couple of them were good'uns too but, in the end, there wasn't enough proof to bring either of 'em before a judge and jury. No. The best one out of the two was a bloke called Leonard Clifford. Oh, clever sod, he was. In my heart, I know he was Jack. I know it. Just couldn't prove it. There was nothing. Still drives me crazy.'

'Oh, you poor thing. I'm so sorry.'

He smiled at her. 'Don't be. It's the way of things some-times. Some get away. Usually the smart ones. And this boy — ' he shook his head — 'this boy was smart. Very smart. Still, all done now. At least he stopped killing, thank God.'

'Stopped? Why?'

'Dunno. Couple of theories. Might have gone to prison for something else for a long time. Might even have been for a murder or something. Funny to think that he's rotting away in a jail somewhere for murder and we can't tie him to my cases. Maybe, and this is most likely, he died. Disease? Accident? I dunno and I don't care. I just hope if it was dis-ease it was painful and took him a bloody long time to die.'

'Bill!'

'Sorry. But . . .'

What's this?' She picked up the old cassette.

'He left these on each of his victims. It's a song called "Mack the Knife." Old song.'

'I know it. Why did he leave this on the bodies?'

'Killers often leave objects or notes on or near their vic-tims. It's their calling card, so to speak. The press jumped on it straight away and called him 'Jack the Knife.' The good old redtops, eh? Can't beat that sort of humour, can you?'

'Weird. Any theories as to why?'

'Not really. It was probably playing in the house when the old man beat seven bells of snot out of him. That's usually the story.'

'Is that what happened to him?'

Bill shrugged. 'As I said, I don't know. We didn't catch him, did we?'

Susan put the photos and cassette back in the suitcase and closed the lid, then picked up the paperback and waggled it at him. 'Can I borrow this, please?'

Bill was curious. 'If you want. But why?'

'Lots of reasons. It would be great to know more about you as a younger man, a dashing DCI in the Met — and this whole investigation. And I'm sure it will be useful as background reading for my own studies. Then I'll come back and pick your brains with lots of questions. Perhaps we can even go over the paperwork together. You can explain to me how an investigation works. You don't mind, do you?'

He felt himself perking up. 'No, not at all. Would be nice to talk about the old days, swing the old blue lamp and all that and, you never know, you might see something in the papers that I've missed. Fresh eyes and stuff.'

She stood up and put the book in her pocket. 'I doubt that very much, Detective Roach of the Yard.' She headed for the door.

'Susan . . .'

She turned back to him. 'Yes, Bill?'

'Stranger things have happened.'

CHAPTER EIGHTEEN

At 4 p.m., Bill shuffled into Mrs Dunbar's office. She rose to greet him, as did a smartly dressed woman in her early sixties.

'Come in, Bill,' said Mrs Dunbar. 'This is Casey, Gillian's daughter.'

'Hello, Mr Roach.' Casey held out her hand. Her finger-nails were short, which didn't seem right on a woman dressed in such a well-cut suit. Short hair . . . no earrings . . . no wedding ring . . . practical watch clasped tightly over a thin wrist.

'I'm Casey. Casey Stevens.' Married name . . . divorced.

Bill sniffed as the woman introduced herself, then held out his hand. She had a firm handshake. It all added up. Cop. He knew one when he saw one. Judging by her age, she was most likely retired.

'Nice to meet you,' he said. He looked away from her and headed for the nearest hard-backed chair.

Mrs Dunbar stood behind him as he struggled to sit himself down. She danced and hovered close to his back, no doubt hoping he wouldn't tumble over. She wouldn't be able to hold him if he did. Bill shuffled about until he was comfortable. Casey Stevens sat back down.

'Casey has a few questions she'd like to ask you about her mother. Are you okay with answering her?'

Bill shrugged. No problem. He raised his head to look at her.

Casey smiled, crossed her legs and leaned forward. She raised her voice a level as she spoke. 'Thank you, Bill. I appreciate you giving me your time.'

Bill nodded. 'Just don't take up too much of it, love. I don't have much left these days.'

She smiled again, broader. 'I'll be as quick as I can. Promise.'

'Go on, then,' he said.

'Mrs Dunbar said you were the last person to see my mother alive. Is that right?'

'Mm-hm.'

'And how was she? How did she seem?'

Bill frowned as he looked her in the eye. 'Well, I'm no expert, Casey, but I'd have to say she looked like she was dying. Come to think of it, she was.'

Casey's smile left her. 'I'm sorry. Silly questions. Of course she was. Just trying to break the ice. Sorry.'

'That's alright, love. It happens. Hope you didn't think me rude? I didn't mean to be.'

Casey shook her head. 'Not at all.' She picked at a bit of lint on the knee of her trousers. 'Let's try again. Obviously, Mum was dying, I knew that, but I wondered if she had said anything to you before . . . y'know . . . before she passed away.'

Bill looked down at the floor for a second before raising his head. 'No. When I went into her, she was asleep. I spoke to her . . . called her name. Nothing. She didn't move.'

'Was she uncomfortable?'

'No, I don't think so. She wasn't in any pain, if that's what you're thinking. None that I could see, anyway.'

Casey nodded. Slowly. 'That you could see?'

'Yes. I mean, she wasn't distressed. Not that I could see.'

'Okay.'

'We do take good care of our patients, I can assure you,' said Mrs Dunbar. 'When it became apparent that your mum was in the last stages, we made sure that she had sufficient

86

care around her. We have nurses here and they looked after her, made sure she was comfortable.'

Casey looked slightly ruffled. 'Oh no, I'm sorry. I wasn't suggesting she wasn't cared for. If it sounded like I was, I apologise. It's just that Mum went downhill so rapidly, and as far as I know, apart from a few bits and pieces going wrong and obvious old age, there wasn't that much wrong with her.'

'Yeah, well, old age'll do it every time,' Bill sniffed.

'He's right,' said Mrs Dunbar. 'Every time. But, to be fair, the things wrong with your mum were quite severe — heart, liver, kidneys . . .'

'Of course,' said Casey. 'Yes. You're right, of course. But I understood she was taking medication for all of those things. To control them.'

Mrs Dunbar nodded kindly. 'Well, yes, she was. That's right. But sometimes the body just gives out.'

'You see a lot of it around here, love,' said Bill. 'It's not nice, but it happens. You get used to it.'

'Bill, Mrs Dunbar had told me that you were with her. Thank you for that, for sitting with her. I really do appreciate it. I . . . I couldn't be there.' She looked at the floor again, then up at Bill. 'Work thing, y'know? Couldn't get out of it.'

Bill pushed his bottom lip out and slowly nodded. He knew. But it wasn't an excuse. And she knew it. 'I'm sorry,' he said. 'You're her daughter, yes?'

Casey tilted her head. 'Sorry?'

'Her daughter. You're her daughter. Correct?'

'Er, yes.'

Bill held his hand up. 'It's alright, don't worry. Not saying anything. Apart from . . . here's a question for you. How long had your mum been in here, in this home?'

'Excuse me?' Casey's tone was slightly defensive.

'How long? How long had she been a resident here?'

'I don't know off the top of my head. Four years . . . five. Why?'

'I know. Five years and three months. You know how I know that? I'll tell you. I liked your mum. She was a lovely lady. Always smiling, laughing. Cared about everyone else. How they were, how they were feeling — can I get you anything? That type of stuff. Was always trying to help. Always . . . so nice, so caring. To everyone. So, when her time came, I wanted to be with her. It was a privilege for me, if that makes any sense.' He glanced over at a very uncomfortable-looking Casey Stevens. She said nothing.

'And in all the time I've been here, in this home, I've never seen you before.' He shook his head. 'Not once. Now, I'll grant you, we could have missed each other once or twice, but I don't think we did, did we? So, you must have had a lot of things going on at work that you couldn't get out of.' He rolled out his hands in an over-to-you gesture.

'Bill . . .' said Mrs Dunbar.

Bill sat there and said nothing.

Casey met his gaze. 'Yeah, you're right. You're right. I didn't see Mum that much—'

'At all?' Bill was digging in for a fight.

'Hmm. At all. But — and this is none of your business — we didn't get on very well. Didn't much get on before, when I was a kid. Definitely didn't when I got married.'

'Was he a wrong'un?' said Bill.

Casey gave him a wry little smile. 'Turned out that way. Anyway, Mum never liked him. Never.'

'Always had a good instinct for people, did your mum. Good at weighing them up.'

'Well, as I said, we didn't get on. We fell out over it. I got on with my life, she got on with hers and that's that. For some reason or other, we never managed to patch it up.'

'Did you try?' said Bill.

Casey rubbed her jaw like she had a toothache. 'Look, I'm sorry, Bill. I know you liked Mum, got on with her, but I didn't, and you have no right to judge me for it. It's none of your damn business what went on in our lives. Let's just say the woman you knew isn't the woman I knew. Okay?'

Bill shrugged. 'Doesn't sound like you knew her at all.'

'Bill!' said Mrs Dunbar. 'Enough.'

Bill glanced over at her, then back to Casey. He spotted a tear in the corner of one eye. That was progress.

She uncrossed her legs and sat up straight. She was fighting back. Bill smiled.

'No more beating around the bush, Bill. You're being with my mum at the end? It's a bit . . . weird, isn't it? I mean, who does that?'

'Well,' said Bill, unfazed, 'people who care about people do.'

Casey nodded. 'Yeah, that's true. Seems you're the caring sort, right? You've sat in on more than a few people just before they died, isn't that right?' Bill could see she was angry.

'Yep. I have. And I'll be there for others until my time comes, and when it does, I hope someone's there to see me out. It's just, y'know, the right thing to do. But, unless I'm wrong, it sounds to me a bit like you're gearing up to accuse me of something. Are you? Because if you are, let's have it. C'mon. Out with it.'

Now Casey was looking frustrated. He'd called her out. She had to answer. 'Okay, okay. I'm just wondering if you've somehow benefitted from these people's wills in some way or another.'

'Mrs Stevens!' protested Mrs Dunbar. 'Excuse me! That's quite enough of that! How dare you come in here and make that kind of allegation against a man who has done nothing but show kindness to people in their dying hours? That's a disgraceful thing to say and you should be ashamed of yourself.'

'Should I?' Casey was up on her feet now. In for a penny . . . 'Has anyone checked?'

'I think it's about time you left,' said Mrs Dunbar. 'I'm not having this any longer.'

Bill held his hand up to Mrs Dunbar. 'It's okay. Thanks for sticking up for me. There's no need, though.' He turned to Casey. 'To answer your allegation, I've not benefitted in any way at all. Please feel free to check. You'll find nothing wrong. Nothing at all. All I've done, all I've ever done, is the decent thing. But, as we're slinging allegations around, let's have a look at you, shall we?

'You pop up out of the woodwork after, what did we say? Oh yeah, five years and three months, pretending to be all concerned and upset. But my money's on you sniffing around for her money, her house. What's that worth, eh? She used to live in Acton, right? Places there aren't cheap, are they? Maybe half a million for her house? One? Two? Told me she had a three-bedder. Paid for her own care here so no one came after the house for care home fees, so that's free and clear. Once the paperwork's sorted — probate, that sort of thing — you'll be rolling in it, won't you?'

Casey Stevens's face and body language made it obvious to him that she was about to blow a gasket. In for a penny . . .

'So, being the lovely daughter you are, you decide you want a post-mortem done. Given her age and the fact she was seen by a doctor before she died — and let's not forget the nursing staff — I can't see any reason you would want her cut up unless it's out of spite. The only other thing I can think of is, you think she might be hiding a bag of jewellery inside her.'

Casey Stevens lost it. 'What? Oh, no. Who the hell do you think you are, you nasty old man? That is so out of order. You should be ashamed, saying things like that.'

Bill shrugged. 'And yet I'm not. You're the one who should be ashamed. You. Cutting your mother up for no good reason.' He looked at Dunbar. He was done with this. 'Just get out of here. I don't want to waste another breath on you. Just go, love. Just . . . go.'

'Oh, no. You don't get to talk to me like that and think you can get away with it.'

'Mrs Stevens,' said Mrs Dunbar, 'enough from you! Get out of here now! I will not have you talking to my residents like that. What's wrong with you?'

Casey looked stunned. 'With me? Are you serious? He says those things to me and I'm the one in the wrong? Jesus! How does that work?'

'I said go. You're not welcome here anymore. Call tomorrow with your address and we'll send your mother's belongings on. Now leave. C'mon, out.'

Looking every bit the wounded daughter, Casey Stevens headed for the door, wrenched it open and stepped out into the corridor. She turned back and glared at Bill. 'Those breaths you don't want to waste on me, I hope you don't have too many left, you horrible old man.'

'Get out!' Mrs Dunbar shouted.

Casey Stevens stormed out of the building, marched across the car park and jumped into her BMW, banging the door loudly.

Bill looked at Mrs Dunbar. 'That went well. I could do with a cuppa.'

CHAPTER NINETEEN

Mrs Dunbar arranged for tea to be brought into the office and she and Bill sat there sipping at it. She wasn't happy with Bill. Bill wasn't happy either. He was the first to break the awkward silence.

'Mrs Dunbar, I'm sorry. I shouldn't have said those things, I know.'

She put her cup down. 'No, Bill, you shouldn't have. It's not for you to judge how people conduct their lives.'

'I know. It's just that people like her get right up my nose. And for her to question me and my motives . . . well, that really upset me, annoyed me.'

Mrs Dunbar softened. 'Yeah, she was completely in the wrong there. You didn't deserve that and it got my goat too. That's why I asked her to leave.'

Bill chuckled. 'Asked her to leave? You slung her out, and good for you. I appreciate you sticking up for me. Thank you.'

Mrs Dunbar shrugged. 'I'll not put up with that kind of behaviour from anyone. She was rude and aggressive. There was no need for it.' She frowned. 'But you did poke the bear somewhat, Bill. The crack about the jewellery was particularly nasty. Clearly, it upset her.'

'I know. I wanted to upset her and, to be honest with you, I'm not sorry I said it. We both know she's come gold-digging and I hate that. I've seen it so many times in here. It's not right.'

Mrs Dunbar nodded. 'You're big on things being done right, aren't you?'

'I am. Look, I know people lead very different lives, of course I do. I'm not stupid. And I know lives can be complicated. I get that too. But what I don't get is that this . . . Casey woman can appear out of the blue when her mother dies but not once, not *once*, did she do it before. She could have at least made the effort to care before she went on the grab. It's wrong.'

'You heard her, though, Bill. They weren't close. It happens. Just because she was her mum, doesn't mean they have to love each other. It's odd, I'll admit, but there we are. That's what happens sometimes.'

Bill shook his head. 'Yeah. It happens. Anyway, it's over now. She knows how I feel. We've both said our piece and that's that. Done.'

'Let's hope so,' said Mrs Dunbar.

Bill perked up. 'What does that mean?'

'Nothing in particular.' She shook her head. 'It's just that I've seen her type before. So many times. She'll complain.'

Bill shrugged. 'Let her. She can't complain about you. You didn't do anything wrong.'

'I was rude and aggressive to her.'

'No, you weren't. You were firm and straight with her. She was being abusive and you just stood up for me in the face of an angry woman who was shouting her head off. That's it. I'll stand by you if she moans about it but I don't think she will. Don't worry about it.'

Mrs Dunbar etched out a small grin, her mug of tea held close to her lips with both hands. 'Thank you, Bill.'

'No worries.'

They sat in silence again for a minute, lost in their own thoughts about what had gone on, before Bill spoke. 'Can I just ask you something?'

'Of course. What is it?'

'Something she said.'

'What?'

'About benefitting from the wills.'

'Hmm?'

'Well . . . look. Something's been bothering me for a while.'

Mrs Dunbar's eyes narrowed. 'Go on.'

Bill sighed. He knew she wouldn't like what he was about to say. 'It's just that, well . . . it's about Dr Cooper.' He looked directly at her. 'Do you think he could . . . y'know . . . could he maybe have benefitted from their deaths?'

Mrs Dunbar looked stunned. 'What? Are you serious?'

'Yeah. Look, I've been thinking about this. For a while. He comes in on his rounds and then usually, within about twenty-four to forty-eight hours, one of us turns our toes up. Don't you think that's strange? I do.'

'What on earth are you talking about? You can't go around saying things like that, you'll get into so much trouble. Do you have any evidence to back this nonsense up?'

'Well, I have been keeping notes of when he turns up and when someone dies. There's a pattern.'

'Look, Bill, that's enough. I don't want to hear this. It's ridiculous.'

Bill gave a nod. Short and sharp. 'Maybe. Maybe not. I'm not so sure it is ridiculous, though. Do you want to look at my notes?'

Mrs Dunbar thrust her hand forward, palm first. 'No. No I don't.'

Bill sighed. 'Okay, but I'm telling you, something's not right and I think you know it too.'

She looked horrified. 'Excuse me?'

'How long has he been here as our doctor?'

Mrs Dunbar shrugged. 'I don't know. Couple of years, maybe. Why?'

'How many years have you owned this place? Lots, yes?'

'Yes. Where are you going?'

'I'll bet I'm right in saying that in the last couple of years, since Cooper came on board, you've lost more residents than in any other two-year period. Am I right?'

He could see that she was shaken. 'Look, I'm sorry, I really am. But if I'm right then we have to do something about this. We can't let this slide.'

Mrs Dunbar stared at him. He watched her chest expand and then hold it in for a few seconds before slowly letting it out with a low whistling noise.

'Bring me your notes tomorrow. We'll have a look together.'

'Y'know, my money's on Cooper, but I wouldn't rule out Draper either.'

'Yeah, that's enough. Goodnight, Bill.'

CHAPTER TWENTY

Bill sat in the lounge watching TV. A large room with high ceilings, it had an enormous picture window that looked out onto the neatly kept garden, itself huge. Both sides of the fence were lined with trees, one of them an apple, and at the end was a shed where the gardener kept his tools. Whatever time of day it was, there was usually someone else in the lounge, often sound asleep, head hanging down. Today there was no one.

He was content with that. People would often complain that they were lonely, despite the number of residents. Bill had no issue with being on his own. Never had. As far as he was concerned, it was good to get some quiet time alone with his thoughts outside the confines of his room. For now, he had the telly to himself, and *Flog It* was on, a half-hour show that pitted two teams against each other to see who could buy things from antique shops and make a quick profit selling them on. All old people liked this, he reckoned.

'Well, well. If it ain't the filth.'

Bill jerked as the grating tone of Jackie Draper shattered his silence. She must have walked in quietly. Either that or his hearing had got worse. She walked around his chair and stood in front of him.

'What do you want?' he asked.

'Me? Nothing. Just thought I'd pop in and see my favourite old coffin dodger. See how you're doing.'

'I'm sorry to upset you, but I'm doing fine. Now let me watch my programme.'

Draper turned and looked at the TV. She turned back and grabbed the remote from the arm of Bill's chair before he could move. 'You don't wanna be watching that crap, Billy boy. You should be watching something about your old mates, the Old Bill. Here! That suits you, don't it? Old Bill. You're Old Bill too. Geddit?'

Bill could feel the tension in the air, like hot static electricity, as he glared at Draper. His argument with Casey Stevens hadn't left him in the mood for Draper's antics. He had reached his limit. He gripped the arms of his chair, rocking himself forward slightly in a vain attempt to signal his intention to leave, when Draper leaned in closer. Bill knew, without a doubt, that he should walk away. But something about Draper's tone made it impossible for him to leave. He felt frozen in place, unable to reply, as she smirked at him.

'Oi! Hold on,' she said, stepping closer, blocking his movement. 'Where'd you think you're going, copper? Don't be going yet. We're having fun.'

Bill sat still. 'You're having fun. I'm not in the mood to play. Let me up, please.'

'No, not yet. I thought I'd give you a taste of your own medicine. See how you like it.'

Bill looked confused. 'What? What're you on about?'

'Being stopped from where you're going to. You coppers do it all the time, don'tcha? Stopping people from going about their business and getting all cocky with them. I know.'

Bill looked into her face and saw her entire life there: hard, uncaring, lifeless eyes; beaten down by a miserable existence; growing up with nothing; mentally slow. Probably had a useless, never-around-much husband who ran off with a council estate teenager with loose knicker elastic, a drug habit and a couple of kids that brought the police to her door from an early age. He'd seen this so many times before. No doubt she had her reasons to despise the police.

'Only if there's good reason for it, Draper. The police don't stop people without cause to.'

'Is that right? Well, you lot are always stopping my two boys wherever they are. Minding their own business, they are, and you lot are all over them like a rash.'

Bill sighed. 'Have they ever been arrested for anything?'

Draper's eyes narrowed. 'What?'

'Have they ever been nicked for anything?'

'Yeah. Why? What's that got to do with anything?'

Bill pushed himself back into his chair. She wasn't going to move and he didn't put it past her to physically stop him if he tried. 'How many times?' He waited for an answer from a slightly confused-looking Draper.

'A few.'

Bill shrugged. 'Ten? Twenty? What?'

It was Draper's turn to shrug.

'And how many times have they been convicted?'

'What's your point, copper?'

'Point is, and you won't like this, but it's only the stupid ones that get caught and only the very stupid get caught multiple times. They're obviously not too quick at learning, are they? So, for the police, they're easy fish. They're the coupla morons they nick when it's pissing down with rain and the cops want to get in out of the wet. That's why they get stopped a lot. That's why they get nicked a lot. Dumb as dirt.'

Draper bunched her fists and set her face into a hard scowl. 'Don't you talk about my kids like that, you old sod. They're bloody good kids.'

Bill snorted. 'Course they are.'

'They don't do nothing wrong. You lot fit them up. Distract them. Put things in their pockets. Make stuff up. I can't stand you. Any of you.'

Bill shook his head. 'Look, take responsibility for them. Clearly, you're no good at being a mum, otherwise they wouldn't be in trouble all the time.'

98

Draper's eyes went wide. That one hurt. 'What did you say? I'm not a good mum?'

Bill grinned slightly and gave a non-committal nod.

'Don't you dare say that about me. Don't you dare!'

Bill had had enough and tried again to lift himself out of his chair again. Draper wasn't having it.

'That's it. I'm done with you. I'm going to make your life a misery from now on. You understand me, old man? A bloody misery.' She stood aside and allowed him to stand up.

'Well,' he said, reaching for his walking stick, 'in all honesty, what's new?' He began to shuffle off.

'That's it, you old fart. Run away. You Old Bill are all the same. Cowards, the lot of yer.'

Without looking back, Bill raised a hand, a dismissive gesture that enraged Draper even more.

'You wait, Bill. I will fuck you up, you'll see.'

Bill headed for the door, muttering to himself as he did so. 'Yeah? Well, let's see, shall we, Draper? Let's just see.'

CHAPTER TWENTY-ONE

At breakfast the next day, Bill rose from his seat and took his mug over to the sink. From where he stood, he could see the main entrance to the building and Mrs Dunbar's office. The two people she was talking to piqued his interest: a man and a woman, early forties, both suited and booted.

Mrs Dunbar looked nervous, and she seemed agitated by their presence. He figured them for police. Seemed to him that Casey Stevens had kicked up and set the dogs on Dunbar. Bitch. It was just a matter of time before he was called into the office. He waited. It gave him a little thinking time before he spoke to them, and thinking time could only be a good thing in these circumstances. He'd learned that a long time ago.

He gave his mug a quick rinse under the tap and put it back in the cupboard above the sink. He kept glancing over to Dunbar's office every once in a while, before plonking himself down in a chair that gave him a square-on view.

As the meeting progressed, he watched Mrs Dunbar relax and knew that the real reason they were there was for him. He'd thrown the proverbial cat into the flock of pigeons and now he would have to face the consequences. But if Casey thought she could intimidate him, she was sorely mistaken. Bill didn't apologise to anyone, especially if he believed he was in the right, and he was most definitely not the type to apologise to someone who ran and got their friends to fight for them.

He could feel his blood boiling as they continued to talk, and he couldn't wait for them to try and extract an apology from him. Nothing he'd said or done was a crime. Let them come. He was ready.

Five minutes later, Mrs Dunbar opened her office door and beckoned him in. She seemed to be quite comfortable, and he felt himself relax a little. He hauled himself up and headed toward her. Her visitors were smiling at him through the office window. He took that as a good sign, but did not take it for granted. These things had a way of going south quickly.

'Good afternoon, Bill.' Mrs Dunbar stood to one side and reached one arm over his head to allow him past her.

Bill nodded. 'Afternoon.'

The two police officers gave him warm smiles and the male officer offered him some help as he sat himself down. He took the help and thanked the officer.

'Hello, Bill,' said the female officer. 'Lovely to meet you. I'm DS Grace Winslet. You can call me Grace. Do you mind if I call you Bill?' She had a nice voice. Polite, firm and not the sing-songy, high-pitched type that grated on him.

'Not at all,' Bill said.

'And I'm DCI Harry Carter,' said the male officer. 'We're from the nick down the road and we've been asked to pop in and have a little chat with you.'

Bill eyed this one up. Decent looking, designer stubble the police allowed these days, a tattoo on his wrist, also allowed now. Smart suit, not overly expensive but nicely cut. Probably tailored. Civilised shoes. He smelled of office.

'About?' said Bill.

DCI Carter took a deep breath with the air of a man with better things to do. 'We had a complaint last night from one of our colleagues, a DS Stevens. She came here to talk to you about her recently deceased mother, Gillian Lake. Says that you were the last person to see her alive and that you spent the night with her. Sorry, let me rephrase. That you sat with her until you were woken in the morning, only to find out that she, Gillian, had passed away in the night.'

'Correct. I did. Yes.'

'And that during the course of the conversation, things got a bit . . . heated between the two of you. Is that correct?'

'Yep.'

DCI Carter nodded. 'I see.'

'What is it you see, Mr Carter?'

Carter cocked his head at the question, clearly unsure of the best way to answer. Bill saved him the trouble.

'We had a row, no denying it. She got arsey about me being in the room for some reason, thought it odd for me to do that. In turn, I got arsey with her about being on the grab.'

'The grab?' said Winslet.

Bill looked at her. She was pretty, nose turned up at the end but only enough to make it cute. Red lipstick. They allowed that these days too. Dark brown hair pulled into a ponytail. He liked a girl with a ponytail. It was a hugely feminine trait. He smiled at her. 'Yeah. The grab, the grab.' He started making a grasping motion with both hands. 'After the money. The house. Grab what you can, y'know?'

Winslet nodded. 'I know exactly what you mean. Had the same thing with some of my relatives a few years back.'

Bill nodded. 'There you go, then. Grabber.' He knew she was most probably feeding him a line. Standard tactic to build empathy. If he saw her as someone who sympathised with his point of view, he'd more than likely open up to her — if it was necessary.

'Anyway,' said Carter, 'that aside, she said that you objected, quite vocally, to a PM being carried out on her mother. It concerned her for some reason.'

'What reason would that be?'

'Well, to be blunt, Bill, it's not really any of your business.'

Bill smiled. 'I know. You're right, it isn't. Look, at the end of the day, it's up to her. She can do what she likes, of course. It's her mum, but I just don't see any reason for it. She was what? Ninety-three? Bound to die at some point in the not-too-distant future, so the only reason she has for doing that, I would think, is that she suspects foul play. Is that right?'

Carter looked at Bill, not accusatory but interested.

'I'm guessing she thinks someone here did for her old mum. Most likely me because she accused me of dipping my fingers in her will—'

'And have you?' Carter interrupted.

Bill gave him a stare. He wasn't amused. 'No. Feel free to dig. Dig as much as you like. I'm eighty-one years old, I have no family and I have a nice little pension that feeds and clothes me. My needs are minimal. I have no interest in her money at all. Gillian was a nice old dear. Kind to everyone. And her daughter got the needle with me because I pointed out that she'd only stopped by once her mum was dead. Her mum brought her into this world, but she couldn't be arsed to see her mum out of it. I don't like it. It's wrong. And I told her. So, go dig as much as you like, Mr Carter. There's nothing to find. But . . .'

Mrs Dunbar frowned.

Bill sat quiet for a few seconds, mulling over whether he should mention his Dr Cooper theory. He decided he would.

'I have a theory, if you're interested?'

'About what?' said Carter.

Bill glanced over at Mrs Dunbar. She gave him a slight nod, picked up by Carter.

'A theory about what, Bill?' Carter repeated.

He looked up at the man. 'Could we all have a nice cup of tea first?'

CHAPTER TWENTY-TWO

Mrs Dunbar's office was small, but now it held an air of importance. Bill was back in control, the centre of attention, just like in the old days. He sipped his coffee slowly, savouring its warmth as he scanned the room. His gaze lingered longest on Grace Winslet, a silent acknowledgement of his respect for her.

'Look . . .' he said. 'I know how this will sound. You'll think I'm mad — or senile probably — but all I ask is that you hear me out, okay? Let me say what I have to say and then you can look into it or not. If you do, I think you'll have a result on your hands. If not, then no harm done. I'll shut up, drop the whole thing and say nothing more. Fair?'

'Hard to say, Bill,' said Carter. 'I have no idea where you're going with this, so I can't say yet. Make a start, eh?'

Bill grinned. 'Fair enough, Mr Carter. I've been here a good few years now, and in that time I took it upon myself to sit with the folk who were dying and had no one to be with them. Just something I wanted to do, y'know? It's not right to me to be on your own in your last moments. I wanted to be there for people.

'So, the way it works here is that we have a local GP assigned to us, to this home. He comes in and gives a few of the sickies the once-over. Sometimes he's called if they've taken a turn or whatever, does his doctor stuff, hands out medicines and then goes. Okay?'

Both officers nodded.

'Okay. Nothing wrong with that, except . . . except I've noticed that since the doctor we have now, Dr Cooper, arrived, there's been an . . . increase, shall we say, in the number of deaths here.'

DCI Carter sniffed and looked at Mrs Dunbar. She gave him a weak smile, neither denying nor confirming.

'What makes you say this, Bill?' said Winslet.

'Something about him, love. Couldn't put my finger on it when he first arrived. Still can't, if I'm honest. So, I kept notes and I think there's a pattern.'

'Notes? A Pattern?' Carter's voice slightly higher in tone. 'Why are you keeping notes on him?'

'I just told you, Mr Carter. There is a rise in the number of deaths.'

'Yeah, but Bill,' said Winslet. 'This is an old people's home. I don't wish to sound disrespectful, but people of this age are not the healthiest, are they?' She looked over at Mrs Dunbar for confirmation. With a slight nod, she got it.

'Mrs Dunbar,' Carter said. 'Is it unusual to see a sharp rise in patient deaths for no apparent reason?'

Mrs Dunbar fidgeted. She clearly didn't want to rubbish Bill but perhaps she hadn't had enough time to compare his notes with her records. Casey Stevens had obviously lost little time in pulling the trigger and the police had probably come in way before she was ready.

'It happens. Not often, but it does. Sometimes there's a perfectly natural explanation for it. Flu at Christmas. Stomach bugs are not friends of the elderly. And, of course, there was Covid-19. Sometimes, it's just an age thing and a few more than normal pass away in relatively quick succession.

'I know some studies have been done that suggest if there's more than three deaths a week in a home like this, it can trigger depressive episodes in some people and they literally give up and . . . die. No one really knows why, I'm afraid.'

'So, why is this any different then, Bill?' said Carter. 'What makes you suspicious?'

'Well, they all died within forty-eight hours of his visit.'

'Ah,' said Winslet, as if it suddenly all made sense.

'I'm going to need to see your notes, Bill,' said Carter. 'And, Mrs Dunbar, the records you keep on all of your residents who've died since Dr Cooper arrived. This chat stays with us in this room, understood? We'll take the information and look into it. That's all I'm prepared to do at this stage. It may be nothing. It may be something. Time will tell.' He nodded curtly. 'Bill, if you could get us your notes before we leave, please. So, if there's nothing else, we'll be in touch.'

Bill nodded. 'No, that's about it. Thanks for not rubbishing my thoughts.'

DS Winslet helped him stand and he left the room.

CHAPTER TWENTY-THREE

'What's that you're reading, Bill?' Susan had walked into the lounge area as he sat in his chair with a book. He looked up when she spoke, always happy to see her. He held it up. 'A true crime story. What else?'

Susan smiled and sat down next to him. Her hair was held back in a ponytail and her smooth skin was pale, a sure sign of the English weather. She reached out delicately to take the book from him, and as she looked at the cover a wide smile spread across her face, like a child who had just received a much-wanted gift. '*The Tiger Strikes*,' she said. '*The True Story of One of America's Worst Serial Killers*. Any good?'

'It's alright. I'm enjoying it. Passes the time away.'

'Good. I hear you've had a bit of a day of it again, Bill. What've you been up to this time?'

He chuckled. 'Me? Nothing. I'm a good boy, I am.'

She smiled at him. 'Oh, I doubt that. You being a detective and all. I'll bet you've gotten yourself into a bit of mischief in your time, eh?'

He chuckled again. 'If you only knew, love. Long time ago, though. Can't turn the clock back. Wish I could. Would have done some things differently.'

'Want to tell me?'

'Can't do that. If I did, I'd have to kill you.'

'Yeah, right, old man. One push and you're flat on your back.'

'Funny girl. I'm sure I'd put up a bit of a fight. Mind you, if I was fifty years younger, I'd be happy to let you push me flat on my back.'

She gave a mock frown. 'Cheeky. That said, looking at the photos of you in that book of yours, I might have been happy to push you on your back.'

Bill felt his grin spread from ear to ear. 'Now who's being cheeky?'

She grinned at him.

'Listen, how you getting on with my book?'

'Not had a chance to read it yet, Bill. Sorry.'

'That's all right, love. I know you're a busy girl.'

'I'm looking forward to it, though. It would be nice to know about you as a younger man, plus it's good for me to read this stuff as part of my studies.'

'Thought you said you're finished with your studies.'

'I have. Technically. But I'm always going to be studying one way or another aren't I?'

'I suppose so. Book's a bit dated, though. Ways of doing things have changed a lot. More technology now. Better databases, systems, communication . . . You name it, it's changed. Can only be for the good, I suppose.'

'Indeed. Just imagine . . . if you had that technology back then, there's no way Jack would have got away with it. Certainly not for so long.'

Bill gave her a rueful smile. 'You don't think so? Don't you believe it. There are still serial killers out there, doing what they do and getting away with it, technology or not. End of the day, catching these people usually comes down to luck. Maybe a random stop on a car and the copper finds a head in a bag, a bloodstained hammer, that sort of thing. Can't beat boots on the street, I always say.'

'Well, I don't know about that, but it's all about the DNA these days, isn't it? I mean, I watch a lot of these forensic detective programs on the telly and from what I can tell, many of these cold cases are getting solved by the boatload now. Every contact leaves a trace and all that.'

Bill scoffed. 'Listen, all that stuff you see on the TV? It's nonsense.'

'Is it? I don't think so, Bill. Things have advanced so much.'

'Yes, I know that. But here's the reality . . . The police find a hair at the scene of a crime. They send it off to the lab. The lab come back with a report — and not within the hour as you see on CSI Miami or whatever — it can take days . . . weeks. And that report might tell you that it belongs to a white male, aged about thirty-five, the nutritional content of his diet and perhaps any significant diseases he's got or had. That hair will also be run through a specialist database looking for a match and then what d'you think happens?'

Susan shrugged. 'They arrest someone?'

'In an ideal world, yes. But that's only *if* they have a suspect in the system with that DNA. What happens if they don't?'

Susan stopped what she was doing. 'I don't know. But that hair will sit on the system, and then one day the murderer will get caught by it. Might be five, ten years, but he will get caught.'

'Until then, he carries on killing. Yes, DNA is a fantastic weapon if you have a suspect to start with or for convicting a suspect if you have one in custody. Other than that, it's just evidence with nowhere to go. If your killer is good at what he does, and Jack was, he'll have left the crime scene and the body clean. And I mean *clean*. He'll have taken extreme care to leave nothing of himself behind, and now, all these years later, what will they find? Nothing on the body because that's long gone. Fibres? What will they match them to now? Any clothing he wore will be long gone. Burned after each kill, I reckon.'

'Hmm. Still, these people do get caught, Bill. Somehow.'

Bill nodded. 'You're right. They do. But that's the amateurs — the friends, the lovers, the family members . . . those desperate for revenge, deranged by jealousy. The professionals, those with knowledge and skill, they don't. Not ever.'

'Well, that makes me feel a lot safer, Bill. Thanks for that.'

The old man chuckled. 'You're welcome, love.' He sniffed and cuffed his nose with the back of his hand. 'I've been thinking. I tell you what, bring my book back. I'll sign it for you and you get to keep it.'

'What? Oh, no. That's not right. I don't want to keep it.'

'No. I insist, Susan. It's no good to me now, is it? I must have read it at least a dozen times. You can keep it as a memento for when I've gone.'

'Bill. Don't say that.'

'What? I've got a lot less in front of me than behind me and that's a fact. No, you have it, love. Maybe, when you've read it, we can have a chat about it. Tell me what you think. Any questions you've got, I'll answer. Be nice to talk about the old days.'

'That would be lovely. Are you sure, though?'

'Sure I'm sure. It would be my pleasure.'

Ten minutes later, Susan was smiling as she read what he'd written on the front page of the book: *To my dearest Susan, thank you for seeing me. With much affection. Your friend, Bill Roach.*

* * *

Once in his room, Bill landed heavily in his chair. How thrilled Susan looked when he handed her the book. She had kissed him on the cheek. Affection — no one had shown him that in . . . He couldn't remember. Fatigue consumed him, causing his eyelids to droop, and he knew he needed a moment of rest. Settling into his chair, he made himself comfortable and closed his eyes. A small tear escaped from the corner of his eye and made its way slowly down his cheek, as he basked in the comfort of Susan's warmth.

CHAPTER TWENTY-FOUR

Julie Dunbar was working in her office. Up to her eyes in paperwork, she was not a fan of Monday mornings. The weekend had brought a few problems that needed her attention. Ivy Peters on the second floor had been sick twice in the night. She would need to see the doctor if it continued. Michael Loon, the name always made her smile, had kicked off with the staff because he didn't want to eat what was on the menu. His Alzheimer's was progressing faster than she cared for. Michael had been a lovely man when he was first admitted, but now the disease was robbing him of his manners and respect, to say nothing of his dignity. Mary Givens on the first floor refused her meds and, given she had a serious heart problem, this had caused the staff no small measure of worry. Thankfully, all the staff knew how best to handle her, and the issue had resolved itself. For now.

Julie shuffled various files around her desk, picking out sheets of paper here and there, stapling two or three together and scribbling little post-it notes to herself. Some went onto sheets of paper, some went onto the cover of a file, one or two made it onto her office window.

She screwed up her eyes and breathed out a long and silent sigh. She really needed help. Cover for the weekend to help take

111

a bit of the load off of her. She doubted she'd get it, though. Shortage of staff was rife in her industry and, as much as it was deemed wrong to say it, Brexit had robbed her of some good, hard-working, caring staff. People who no longer felt wanted or valued in this country. Now she had to employ the likes of Jackie Draper, much to her dismay. She'd already noted an unofficial complaint from one of the weekend staff about Draper's brusque manner with both staff and patients. Letting her go would push the rest of the staff to breaking point, a point they were teetering on now. She'd also have to have a gentle talk with Susan. As lovely as the girl was, she needed to spend less time talking to patients and more time grafting.

Julie glanced up at the clock that hung above her door: 9.15 a.m. It was going to be a busy day and a long week. A tap on the office door startled her.

'Come in,' she called.

The door opened and Bill shuffled his way in. Her heart sank. *Not now, Bill. Give me a break.* 'Good morning, Bill. I'm afraid I'm up to my eyeballs at the moment. Is it important?' Perhaps this was being a little rude, but she hoped he'd had enough Monday mornings in his the past to understood her position.

'Good morning. I'm sorry to bother you when you're busy. I won't keep you a moment. I was just wondering if you'd heard anything from the police yet about Dr Cooper? It's been a while now and . . . nothing.'

She looked up from her paperwork. 'Nothing yet. Sorry. I expect these things take time. I'm sure you know all about that.' She put her head back down and glanced at a report before pushing it to one side and then skim reading another.

'Yeah. It does take time, but I thought you would have heard something by now.'

'I haven't, Bill. I promise you.' She stopped working again. 'Thinking about it, though, why would they tell me anything? I mean, they might tell me when — *if* — he gets arrested, but I'm sure they won't tell me anything while they're investigating. Would you have done?'

112

Bill shrugged. 'That's fair. No, I don't suppose I would have. Alright. I'll leave you to it, then.' He started to back out of the doorway.

She sighed. 'I'm sorry, Bill. I don't mean to brush you off, but I genuinely haven't heard a thing and Monday morning is never the best time to come and talk. Come back this afternoon, after lunch if you like, and we can chat then.'

Bill waved away the offer. 'It's okay. It's not important. Just wondered. I'll see you later in the day when you're around. See you later.'

* * *

Bill closed the door behind him and walked out into the corridor. He stopped, checked his watch and, after a long beat, made a decision.

CHAPTER TWENTY-FIVE

In the week following Carter and Winslet's visit to Mrs Dunbar, Jackie Draper had been wary of Bill. His retort had taken her aback. The other residents were used to her bullying and harassment, and they all avoided her. She was used to getting her own way and not being challenged. Bill's words had thrown her, but the look in his eyes had startled her even more — it was a look of defiance that she hadn't seen in anyone for a long time. She wanted to know more about this side of him that he had never shown, but for the time being, she kept a distance from him. This allowed her time to make someone else's life more difficult instead.

* * *

As for Bill, enough was enough. He was preparing to make good on his personal goal of making Jackie Draper's life difficult. His walking stick sounded like a crutch as he made his way up the small set of concrete steps with the help of a metal handrail. He refused the offer of help from an officer leaving the station and clung to the rail. The cold metal bit into the palms of his hands as he struggled his way up the steps. The officer held the door open for him, and caught Bill as he stumbled slightly on the way in.

'You okay, sir? Should have let me help you up.'

Bill looked into the young man's eyes. 'I'm okay, young-ster. Thank you, though. I appreciate the offer.'

* * *

The main foyer of the police station was empty. He approached the desk and looked around the station. It was one of the few remaining original police stations in London. All the rest had been sold off to developers for conversion to luxury flats and the money used to build new 'super-stations'. In reality, these new stations were just custody suites in office blocks. He couldn't see the need for shiny new offices that smelled of carpet and polish. These were not police stations. Stations, in his memory, all had high ceilings, old oak counters with a hinged flap for entry and exit, floors covered in some kind of plastic tile — slippery when wet. A large wooden desk would face the counter where the station officer sat. Tall sash windows and walls were painted in various shades of beige and cream. Off to the side would be the charge room, and another big desk for the custody sergeant to book in prisoners and an area where fingerprints were taken. A solid block of brass would be covered in ink with a small rubber roller. The fingers were then pressed onto the ink and individually rolled across a fingerprint form, hopefully without any smudges. That was proper, not the electronic gadgetry they used these days. This wasn't his world anymore.

He looked at the counter of this police station: lami-nate, scarred from a few years of abuse, with chipped wooden edges. In the corner was a little printed sign, its edges curling up where the old, yellowed Sellotape had lifted and brought the paper up with it. *Press for assistence*, it said. The spelling mistake infuriated him. The sign had been there for some time so why had no one corrected it? No standards anymore.

He shook his head in dismay and pressed the button a few seconds longer than he should have.

A bald-headed man in his fifties poked his head out of a side office. 'Won't be moment, sir, and I'll be with you.' Bill frowned at the accent. American? Canadian maybe? God help us.

He looked around at the walls of the office. There was still the usual array of wanted posters, villains who were on the run. He looked at one in particular, a miserable-looking man in his thirties with a beard that needed a good trim. He had a unibrow that reminded him of a two caterpillars having sex. There was a scar above his right eyebrow and the fact that one eye was slightly lower than the other topped off the whole presentation. Bill read his name, couldn't pronounce it, and shrugged.

'Yessir, how can I help you?' The bald man had finished what he was doing and was standing at the counter, beaming a smile. His teeth weren't bad, fairly even and white. He wore a blue V-necked jumper over a pale blue shirt. His name badge read, *John Tenant Customer Assistant*. Bill shook his head. In his day there were no badges and these people would have been coppers, not civilians and certainly not 'customer assistants'. He shook his head again.

'I'd like to see DS Grace Winslet, please. She's not expecting me but tell her it's Bill Roach. Old Bill from the home. She knows me.'

'I'll give her a try for you, by all means. Would you like to take a seat while you wait? It might take me a few minutes to track her down. I don't know if she's in the station or out.' John Tenant opened a door his side of the counter and then opened a door on Bill's side. It led to a small waiting room with a desk and three chairs.

'Thanks,' said Bill and he shuffled into the office. He took a seat while Tenant picked up the phone and dialled the main CID office.

The room smelled a bit off to him. Bodies. There was no disinfectant. Disgusting. As he looked around, he spotted what looked like a small patch of blood smeared on the wall. It cheered him up, thinking that someone had stepped out of line and got his come-uppance. Perhaps proper policing wasn't quite dead.

Two minutes later, smiling customer assistant John Tenant opened the door. 'You're in luck, sir. She was at her desk. She's on her way down to see you now. Should be a couple of minutes. Would you like a tea?'

Bill frowned. Tea? *This is a police station, son, not a bloody café.* 'No, thanks. You're alright, son.'

Sure enough, three minutes later, DS Winslet, dressed in dark trousers and a white blouse, entered the room also smiling from ear to ear. She was carrying a folder of papers. 'Bill! How are you?'

Bill smiled back. She was a pretty one. Fifty years ago, she'd have been fighting him off for sure. 'Hello, Grace. I was just passing by, love, and thought I'd poke my head around the door. See what's happening with Dr Cooper. It's been a while.'

Winslet pulled out a chair and sat down opposite Bill.

'Is that his file?' said Bill.

'What? These? Oh, no. They're for my benefit. It's an old cardboard folder full of blank paper. Makes me look busy.' She giggled like she was letting him in on some forbidden secret.

Bill knew how that worked. He'd seen it done so many times, everywhere he'd ever worked. He didn't approve of it, but he'd done it himself so couldn't say anything. 'So, what's happening, then?'

Winslet put the folder down on the desk. 'All I can tell you is that we're looking into things and we'll see where we go from there. You know how it is.'

'Hmm, yeah. But you can give me a nod, can't you? Let me know if you've dug up anything on him?'

'Nope. Can't do that. Wouldn't do even if I could. This is a tricky one, Bill. You've made an allegation against a well-respected doctor, a pillar of the community, so this is all being done sensitively. Quietly.'

Bill frowned. 'Does that mean you're not looking that hard? Because he's a pillar of the community? So was Dr Shipman and Jimmy Savile. Right pair of crafty gits they turned out to be, eh?'

Winslet looked annoyed. 'Er, no, Bill. That's not what I said, nor is it what's going to happen either. We're doing our job and it doesn't mean I tell you what's happening.' Her tone was a little more edged, sharp.

Bill picked up on it. 'I'm sorry, love. I didn't mean anything by it. Just impatient. I don't like the fact that he could still be at it.'

'It's alright, Bill. I'm sorry too. Didn't mean to bark at you. Busy day. If anything happens, you'll know. But in the fullness of time and not before. Okay?'

'Okay. Worth a try, wasn't it?'

'Hmm,' she said. 'Is there anything else?'

Bill sniffed. 'Yeah. If it turns out it's not him, I've got someone else for you.'

Winslet frowned. 'Someone else? What d'you mean *someone else*?'

'Well, you might want to take a look at a carer who works there. Agency woman. Spiteful bitch by the name of Jackie Draper. Really unpleasant woman who goes around making people's lives a misery. She's got two boys — they'll be in your system. Right pair of hooligans — nicking things and selling and dealing drugs. She's definitely worth a look if it's not him.'

He could see from her face she wasn't happy with this new information. It opened up a whole new can of worms, and one can at a time was usually enough. 'Why didn't you mention this before, Bill?'

'Don't know, really. I mean, I do. I still think it's Cooper without a shadow of a doubt but, y'know, I *might* be wrong. And, if I am, then Draper's my second-best suspect.'

Grace stood up, scraping the chair back on the tiled floor. 'Your *second best suspect*? Christ, Bill, this isn't a game of Cluedo. This is people's lives here. If I find out you've made a false allegation against Cooper, for whatever reason, I will come down on you. Hard. You understand me?'

Bill lowered his head and his voice. 'I haven't made a false allegation. I haven't. I honestly believe it's him. But, if it turns out it's not, then it might be her. It could even be both of them. In it together. He gets what's in the will and they split it. Could be, couldn't it?'

Winslet sighed and softened her stance. Maybe she'd found out he was an ex-copper, or more likely she pitied him as a lonely old man living out his limited time in a home, no longer wanted or useful.

'Okay. I'll look into it, Bill. I promise. Go and do what you need to do, shopping maybe. But then go home. Leave it with me. I'll add her as a suspect and look into her if Cooper falls through.'

Bill was somewhat cheered by this. 'Alright, love. Thank you.'

* * *

Grace Winslet helped him to his feet, showed him out the station, walked him down the stairs and watched him toddle off toward the home. She rubbed her face and made a mental note to talk to Mrs Dunbar. Worth seeing if Bill had some form of Alzheimer's.

CHAPTER TWENTY-SIX

Had Gillian Lake still been able to, she would have complained bitterly about the cold metal pressing against her skin and died at the embarrassment of lying naked on a table for strangers to stare at her. Her pitifully thin corpse lay bare under the harsh lights. A long ugly line ran the length of her body from pelvis to collarbone that opened out into a Y shape toward her painfully thin shoulders. The pathologist, Dr Jeanne Armstrong, remarked to her assistant, Paul Carren, that Gillian's skin was so thin as to be almost transparent. She almost added that they didn't need to open her up because a bright light should let them see through her skin, but her humanity and professionalism suppressed her gallows humour. She was getting ready to end the post-mortem when something occurred to her that stopped her in her tracks.

'You all right?' said Paul Carren.

'Just had a thought,' said Jeanne.

From no other source than years of experience in looking for the cause of death in hundreds of corpses, she felt the sudden urge to turn Gillian over again and look a bit closer at her neck. She took hold of her shoulder and asked Paul to help get her over. Thankfully, the cadaver weighed so little that it was an easy task. With Gillian flat down on her face,

Jeanne pulled down the halogen ring light that was attached to an extendable arm above her head.

* * *

'What's up, Doc?' With a thick line of menthol vapour rub under his nose, DCI Harry Carter stood well back from the table. He'd been to more than his share of post mortems in his time, and even though this was a straightforward examination with no obvious sign of injury, he knew that Gillian Lake would be opened up and her insides exposed, hence the greasy moustache he was sporting. The smell of a human being's insides was not one that could be easily forgotten.

Every PM he attended reminded him of a rough-and-ready copper he'd run across once, name of Johnny Clocks. The two had crossed paths on a murder case a few years back and both were in attendance at the victim's post-mortem. An irreverent man, Clocks called the insides of people 'giblets', and that bit of humour broke the tension of the situation. It stuck with him. And now, whenever he attended a PM, he heard Johnny Clocks's voice in his head. It always made him smile and made this whole job a bit more bearable — that and menthol vapour rub. Still, he'd expected he'd be in and out in about thirty minutes or so. Job done. Back to the nick. Cup of tea.

'Just a hunch, Harry,' said Dr Armstrong. 'Gimme a minute, please.'

Pulling the light lower, she slipped on her magnifying glasses to help her examine the deceased more closely. Carter stood to one side to get a clearer view. The nasty stuff was over. Looking at the back of a corpse was easy.

Dr Armstrong pushed back the thin whispers of hair on Gillian Lake's neck and looked at her for a full minute, occasionally pulling the skin from side-to-side and pulling hairs away from her neck.

'Doc?' said Carter.

'Come here, Harry. Take a look at this for me.'

'What? What is it?'

'Take a look.'

Assistant pathologist Carren handed him a pair of magnifier glasses and he joined Dr Armstrong.

'There. See it?' She pointed to an area on Lake's neck.

Carter peered closer. 'Really?'

'Looks like it.'

'Jesus!'

'Indeed.'

'Paul,' she said. 'Take a look, please.'

Carren bent over and looked at the point where Armstrong was still holding the hair up. 'Hypodermic?'

'Hypodermic,' said the doctor.

'Jesus!' said Carter, again.

On the side of the metal table was a red button that activated a digital recorder, used to record findings and afterwards to make up notes. Dr Armstrong checked the recorder was still recording and began to speak.

'I determined to re-check the back of Mrs Lake's neck. Upon closer inspection, I detected a small puncture wound just underneath the hairline, which I believe at this moment to have been caused by a hypodermic needle. My assistant, Paul Carren, has also examined the body and concurs. Further examination of Mrs Lake's body will be necessary, but at this moment I will request a full blood and toxicology report to determine cause of death. As of now, I strongly suspect Mrs Lake to have been the victim of some form of criminal action. Detective Chief Inspector Harry Carter from Leman Street police station is in attendance and was shown the wound. DCI Carter is aware of all relevant details and I am advocating a thorough police inquiry be conducted.'

She pressed the button to stop recording, snapped off her rubber gloves, binned them and began removing her plastic apron. 'Harry?'

'What?' He reached into his pocket and pulled out his phone. He was planning on calling DS Winslet.

'You said earlier when you arrived that Dr Cooper was your suspect for this, is that correct?'

He nodded.

'Can I suggest you bring him in sooner rather than later. God know what else he could be up to.'

Carter nodded and put the phone to his ear. 'Grace?' he said. 'It's me. Round up the troops. We're going after Cooper. Now.'

CHAPTER TWENTY-SEVEN

Dr Cooper was behind his desk when they came for him. DCI Carter, DS Winslet and five other police officers had entered the doctor's surgery and announced their identities. Carter told the young receptionist that they needed to speak to Dr Cooper as a matter of emergency. Although she seemed alarmed by their sudden entrance, it did not faze her. This sort of thing happened from time to time and she figured they needed him to help them with a case, perhaps a murder scene or something. The human mind has a tendency to rationalise things that are out of the ordinary and put them into a safe compartment, one that makes sense, and Dr Cooper giving help to the police was no doubt the natural explanation for this young lady to muster up.

Alarm bells only started ringing for her when Carter told her they were going through and she was not to alert him of their presence.

'B-but . . . h-he has a patient with him. You c-can't . . . can't just go in. H-he'll be furious.'

Carter smiled. 'Well, I'm somewhat pissed off myself, miss. I'm sure we'll both get over it. Who's he with?'

The young woman tapped at her computer. 'Mrs Allwyn.'

'Gracie, you go first,' Carter said.

'Yes, guv.' DS Winslet turned to the young woman. 'What room's he in?'

'Four. T-turn left . . . along the corridor.'

'Johnson,' said Carter, 'stay on the main door. No one else comes in until we're done. Okay?'

DC Johnson nodded. 'Sir.'

The remaining officers, headed by Winslet, followed by Carter, left the reception and headed for Cooper's room.

'No calls, understand?' Carter said to the receptionist as he followed his officers. She nodded.

In the waiting room, Carter surveyed four patients who looked on curiously as the group of police officers headed for the doctor's surgery. 'Anyone here waiting to see Dr Cooper?'

Two hands went up.

'You're gonna have to make new appointments, I'm afraid. Doc's going to be busy elsewhere for a while.'

One of the two, a man, looked genuinely annoyed and wasn't afraid to show it. 'Oh, for Chrissake's! I had to queue up outside for forty-five minutes for the chance to see him, or anyone. D'you know how difficult it is to see a doctor these days? Bloody nigh on impossible, mate. This is a joke.'

Carter sighed and shrugged. 'Yeah, I know. Sorry about that, but what can you do?'

'You can go out and catch a few murderers, mate. That'd help.' The man got out of his chair and, pulling his coat on, glared at Carter.

'Solid career advice there, sir,' said Carter. 'I'll keep it in mind. Thank you.'

The man shook his head and disappeared into the reception area. Carter walked off to join his team. He heard a knocking sound coming from the end of the corridor, saw Winslet at what he assumed was Room 4 and then saw the door being opened. He watched as Winslet spoke to the man who opened the door. By the time he got to his little group of officers, Winslet was inside Cooper's surgery, door left ajar, talking to Cooper's patient, a middle-aged woman who looked totally confused at what was happening. Winslet ushered the woman up and out of the room and turned her attention to Cooper.

'Stay here for a minute, chaps,' Carter said. 'I'll let you know what to do in a minute.' He stepped inside the room.

Cooper's face was a mixture of anger and bewilderment. Carter was quick to put him out of his confusion. 'Dr Sean Cooper?'

Cooper nodded.

'I'm Detective Chief Inspector Harry Carter. This is Detective Sergeant Grace Winslet. Dr Cooper, can you confirm for me that you work over at the Crown Woods Retirement Home?'

'What's this about? Why have you come barging into my surgery? What's going on?'

'Can you answer the question, please?'

'Yes. Yes, I do.'

'Thank you. Did you certify the death of an elderly resident, Mrs Gillian Lake, on the second of this month?'

'What? Mrs Lake? Er, yes, I think so. I'd need to check. Why?'

Carter ignored his questions. 'And did you make your usual visit to the home a day or so before Mrs Lake died?'

Cooper looked very worried at this point. 'What? Why?'

'Yes or no, please, Doctor.'

'Yes, I believe I did.'

'Did you see Mrs Lake then?'

Cooper nodded. 'I did. What's happened?'

'Earlier today, I came from Mrs Lake's post-mortem, requested by her daughter. The pathologist found something . . . unusual, shall we say.'

'Unusual? What'd you mean *unusual*? I don't understand. Look, tell me what's going on here! I demand to know.'

Carter smiled. 'I wouldn't demand anything, sir. You're not really in a position to.'

'The pathologist found something on her body,' said Winslet.

Cooper looked over at her. He'd forgotten she was there. 'Found what?'

'A teeny-tiny hole,' said Carter. 'A needle mark. On her neck. Just under her hairline. Wouldn't have noticed it ordinarily, it's just that this pathologist is good — *very* good. She found it.'

Cooper's face fell. His eyes widened and his legs wobbled under him. He caught himself on his desk and steadied himself.

'Do you want to tell me how that little needle mark got there, Doctor?'

Cooper said nothing, just stared glassy eyed at Carter.

Carter nodded. 'Sean Cooper . . . I'm arresting you on suspicion of the murder of Mrs Gillian Lake on or about the second of March 2023. You do not have to say anything. But it may harm your defence if you do not mention, when questioned, something which you later rely on in court. Anything you do say may be given in evidence. Do you understand what I've just said?'

Cooper said nothing.

Carter looked at his watch. 'The time is 10.47 a.m. The suspect made no reply.

Winslet nodded.

'Okay, Dr Cooper,' said Carter. 'Here's what's going to happen now. We're going to shut the entire surgery and take you out of here. I'm going to leave an officer to ensure no one goes into your office. Later today, we'll conduct a full search of it. We'll run you over to Leman Street police station where you'll be formally interviewed. You can, of course, have a solicitor present. Before we go there, we're going to take you home and we're going to conduct a search of your home. We're looking for anything that may have been used in the unlawful death of Mrs Lake and we'll also be looking for any evidence that you may have been involved in the death of other elderly residents. Do you understand?'

Cooper stared ahead as if unseeing.

'Dr Cooper, do you understand?'

'Home?'

'Yes, sir,' said Carter. 'Your home.'

Cooper swivelled his head to look at Carter. 'No . . . Please . . .'

Carter glanced over at Winslet. She frowned back at him.

'No? Why's that?'

'Not my home.'

'Something there you don't want us to find, Dr Cooper?'

Cooper's eyes welled up. 'Please . . .'

DS Winslet took hold of Cooper's arm. 'Okay, Dr Cooper, we have to go now. This way, please.' With her other hand, she gestured toward the doorway. Cooper complied. He walked like a zombie along the corridor, past his receptionist, and climbed into the back of Carter's unmarked police car.

Carter, meanwhile, instructed one of his officers to ensure no one went into Cooper's surgery until a qualified search team arrived. Then he pulled the surgery door closed and walked off to join Winslet and Cooper. He already had a search team prepped and waiting for him outside Cooper's home address.

CHAPTER TWENTY-EIGHT

Bill was sitting in the restroom when news of Dr Cooper's arrest broke on the local news station. Susan was pottering around talking to other residents, doing a bit of dusting here and there and generally making herself busy.

Bill sat forward when he saw Cooper's face fill the screen. He tuned himself in to what the newscaster was saying.

'Dr Cooper, the senior doctor of a local surgery, was arrested earlier today on suspicion of causing harm to his patients. At the moment, there are no further details available. We'll bring you further information later this evening in our ten o'clock update.'

'Susan! Come over here and listen to this. Quick!'

Susan looked up from what she was doing and ambled over to Bill. 'What's the matter?'

Bill pointed to the screen. 'Come on, hurry up! They've got him!'

'What? Who? What're you talking about?'

'Dr Cooper. He's been nicked. Got the bugger!'

Susan stood next to his chair as the newscast showed various shots of the local surgery and the same photo of Dr Cooper that he had seen earlier. 'Oh, God, I hope it's not true. He was such a nice man.'

'Yeah. So was Harold Shipman.'

'Who?'

Bill tore his eyes away from the TV. 'Shipman. He was the local GP that did home visits and ended up topping his patients.'

'Did he? How many?'

I think he was convicted for . . . I think it was fifteen.'

'Fifteen! My God, that's awful!'

'That's what they convicted him for. Police believe he did at least 250. The biggest serial killer in modern times. Beat the yanks on that one. For a little while, anyway.'

'Bill! That's awful. Don't make fun out of it.'

'I wasn't. But I'll tell you what *is* awful . . . a criminal psychiatrist who hasn't heard of him. What have they been teaching you all this time?'

She ignored him. 'Do you think they have a case?'

He looked back at the TV. 'I should hope so. Those two coppers weren't fools. DS Winslet seems smart enough and, come to that, so does Carter. Yeah, they wouldn't have nicked him if they didn't have something solid. I reckon they've got him bang to rights. Going to be interesting to see how this plays out over the next few weeks.'

'Those poor people! I wonder how many people he killed?'

'Time will tell. I'll be back later to catch the evening news. Will you be here?'

She shook her head and checked her watch. Just gone six. 'I'm off in a minute and thank God for it. I'm so tired.'

Bill chuckled. 'Good for you. Go home and have a bath and an early night. It'll do you good.'

'Too right. Bath and a bottle of dry white. That's me for the night.' She took one last look at the TV and shook her head. 'His poor family. They're the ones who'll have to live with this. It'll ruin their lives too.'

'Yeah. There's always more than one type of victim in any murder.'

'G'night, Bill. Get some rest yourself.'

'Night, Susan. See you tomorrow.'

He settled back in his chair and flicked through the channels. Maybe it was already on other news outlets — BBC, Sky. He spent the next five minutes going up and down through the channels but with no luck. He felt disappointed that nobody else had the story yet, but they would. Locals usually broke a story first and then it got picked up by the big boys. It would soon be all over Twitter and Facebook. The public loved a good murder, and a possible Shipman Number Two? Well, that would be too good to be true. He could see the debates now, especially after the General Medical Council made so many changes to procedures to ensure this sort of thing never happened again. And yet . . . the same thing happened again.

Bill drifted off into a fantasy where he was back in the spotlight, people firing questions at him: How could this have happened? When did he first suspect? Was it him who tipped off the police? He smiled then snapped himself back to reality. No. He didn't want those scum pecking at him. Not again.

He pulled himself slowly out of his chair, took his walking stick and set off to the dining room. There was a good chance Charlie was in there, cup of tea and a packet of biscuits in hand. He wanted to break the news to him. *See, Charlie? You didn't believe me. I was right, wasn't I?*

CHAPTER TWENTY-NINE

The interview room was located in the basement of a former apartment building that had been converted into an office complex. The echoing noises of the restless city outside were barely audible, making it feel like the whole world had shrunk to this one place. The room was large and air conditioned and evenly illuminated by four square lights embedded into the ceiling. There were no windows. A big, round cherry-wood table stood in the centre of the room with two chairs on each side of it. The table and chairs had a glossy finish, making them appear pristine. Seated on one side of the table with his solicitor, Dr Sean Cooper looked terrified. He stared at the table and at the strong metal arch bolted to it, used to secure handcuffed prisoners to the desk to stop them lashing out at the police. It wasn't necessary for him.

Behind the mirror adorning one wall was another room, invisible to the naked eye, but everyone knew it was there. One-way mirrors were a staple of TV crime thrillers.

The room was full of audio and video recording equipment. The panels of LED lights on the voice pattern analysers danced busily up and down as the microphones picked up sounds coming from the interview room. Its job was to look for spikes in the conversation, giving hope to the analysing officer seated in front of it, an indication that Cooper might be lying in places.

Cooper's solicitor opened his case and took out his note-pad and pen, both of which he arranged neatly in front of him. Opposite him, DCI Carter and DS Winslet made their own preparations for the interview. Papers were shuffled, notebooks and pens fiddled with. DS Winslet pushed forward a closed A4 manilla envelope. Inside were close-ups of Gillian Lake's neck, complete with puncture mark.

When everybody had settled, DCI Carter looked at the digital clock on the wall — 6.04 p.m. — and nodded. 'Good evening. My name is Detective Chief Inspector Harry Carter. Other persons present are?'

'Detective Sergeant Grace Winslet,' said Winslet.

'Laurence Bains, solicitor from Bains and Egerton.'

'Sean. Sean Cooper. *Dr* Sean Cooper.'

'Thank you,' said Carter. 'Okay, Sean, you were arrested today at your surgery on suspicion of the murder of Mrs Gillian Lake, a resident of the Crown Woods Retirement Home. Is that correct?'

Cooper kept his eyes downward. 'My solicitor has advised me to make no comment.'

'You have been working as a visiting GP to the Crown Wood retirement home for . . . how long?'

'No comment.'

'Did you know Mrs Gillian Lake?'

'No comment.'

'Rhetorical question. I know you did. When was the last time you saw her?'

'No comment.'

'It was approximately thirty-six hours before she died. You went into her room because she had been feeling very poorly and you were asked to look in on her by Mrs Dunbar, the home's manager. Correct?'

Silence. Then, 'No comment.'

'Did you examine her?'

'No comment.'

'Were you alone when you examined her?'

'No comment.'

'My information is that you were alone when you examined her. What was your diagnosis of Mrs Lake after you examined her?'

'No comment.'

'Were you of the opinion that she might be in the end stages of life? That she might need to be hospitalised?'

'No comment.'

The officers next door in the observation room were not too impressed by the way this was going. No comment interviews never sat well with a jury if it should come to trail. Carter would let Cooper know that when the time was right.

'When you left her, how did she seem in herself?'

'No comment.'

'Okay,' said Carter. Let's move on a bit, shall we? Once you were arrested, you came with us to your home address, where we met up with a professional search team and a forensic search team and they took possession of . . . ' He looked over at the mirror. An officer inside clicked on a photo on his screen and it appeared instantly on the monitor in the interview room.

'Exhibit HC/005 is an Apple laptop computer, found tucked away behind some books on the bookshelf in your home office.'

More images filled the screen. Pictures of the laptop in situ behind the books. 'Can you tell me why it was there, Dr Cooper? Seems an unusual place to keep a fairly new and expensive-looking laptop.'

Cooper fidgeted, not unnoticed by Carter and presumably Winslet and all the officers in the observation room. The camera operator closed in on Cooper's face just as he licked his lips. Dry mouth.

'No comment.'

'Looks to me like you'd hidden it for some reason. Would you like to tell me why you'd hidden it?'

'No comment.'

Carter nodded. 'Okay, you had your chance.'

'I'm sorry?' said Bains, the solicitor. 'Is that a threat, DCI Carter? It certainly sounded like one.'

'Apologies. It wasn't meant to be, Mr Bains. Just that I know what's on it, so I thought it only fair to give Mr Cooper here a chance to tell me for himself.'

'If you know what's on it, Mr Carter,' said Bains, 'then you don't need to ask, do you?'

Carter held his hands up. 'Of course I do. You know I do. But, just thought I'd offer. No problem.' He looked over at Cooper, who made no expression. 'It's just that, sometimes, Sean, it helps to get these things off of your chest, y'know?

'We also seized another laptop, a couple of hard drives and, of course, your desktop computer. Is there anything on any of these you want to tell me about? Any unauthorised paperwork, perhaps? Any . . . pictures? Videos, perhaps?'

Cooper's eyes watered and his fidgeting increased. 'No . . . no comment. No comment.'

'Okay,' Carter said. 'If you're only going to say "no comment" all the time, we might as well shelve the interview for now until you've had a chance to rethink your position.' He looked across to the mirror. 'Interview terminated at six . . . eleven. Dr Cooper, we're going to return you to your cell now, where you'll be held pending further enquiries.'

Cooper looked shocked. Bains had most likely told him he'd be bailed.

'Why are you holding him, Mr Carter?' Bains looked annoyed.

'I just said. Further enquiries.'

'How long do you intend to keep him for?'

'Depends. I need to investigate this matter more fully, as I'm sure you appreciate. You briefing him to "no comment" everything isn't the most helpful advice, I have to say. Still, it's done now.'

'This is wrong. Dr Cooper is a pillar of the community. This will destroy his reputation.'

Carter sighed. 'If it turns out he killed Gillian Lake, the ruin of his reputation will be the least of his worries.'

CHAPTER THIRTY

Susan Johnson's flat was tiny. Small was all she could afford on her salary as a care home worker. Looking after people, while a noble thing to do, wasn't much good for paying the bills. The flat consisted of one bedroom, one bathroom with a shower, and a tiny kitchen. She kept it clean and tidy with a place for everything. She'd always been of the mindset that the key to a happy life was simplicity and, even though she sometimes envied people who had more space, she was happy with her home. It was big enough for her and gave her the space she needed to breathe.

Nursing home employment was never a lifetime career in Susan's eyes. She had merely taken it on as a means to an end: getting a job to buy a home. Unfortunately, the workload had intensified over the last couple of years due to staff shortages and she found herself more and more involved, less able to pull away. Even with all these obligations, she still managed to find the time to study for a degree, a feat that her parents found amazing given that they had warned her multiple times that she was biting off more than she could chew. Nevertheless, her stubbornness and ambition remained stronger than ever.

She'd arrived home just after seven, carrying a bag with her evening meal: Chinese lemon chicken, chicken balls and a portion of noodles. She sat and ate from her lap on the sofa while flicking through Netflix. Her 'My List' had about a hundred things to watch in it, but she just couldn't find anything that pulled her in enough to devote her evening to. She watched a single episode of *Ozark* before throwing her food cartons in the bin and ambling off to the bathroom.

She looked at the time on her phone: 9.57 p.m. There were a number of text messages waiting for her. Unlike most people her age, she wasn't a slave to her phone. She used it as a tool that served her and not the other way around. Her friends and family all knew she wasn't one for social media or texting, so if she didn't get back to them for a few hours, no one panicked. She wandered back into the living room while the bath was running and poured herself a large glass of white wine before heading back to the bathroom.

Forty minutes later, she was lying on her bed with Bill's book. She opened the cover to where he had written his inscription and ran her finger across it fondly. She liked him a great deal, always found him to be a kind. An image flashed into her mind of Draper and the way she treated him, and it angered her. Not wanting to end the day on a low, she pushed the vision out of her head and settled down to read. Another glass of white — smaller — did its bit to help her relax.

Whenever she read a biography, she always turned first to the middle section of the book where it generally contained a section of various photographs from the person's life. Bill's was no different: childhood photos first, his school photo, one with his mum and dad on holiday in Cornwall, a group photo from Hendon police college, a picture of him in his early twenties as a detective sergeant, a couple of crime scene shots and a single photo of a crime report when he was a DCI. The report showed details of the victim, Linda Bowery, her age and a written report from Bill, signed and dated at the bottom. The last photo was of Bill receiving the Queen's Police Medal for Bravery. According to the caption, this was his not his first award. He'd received many commendations for his work as a police officer.

She smiled. The old man she knew had had such an interesting life and a career marked out by so many accolades. It upset her that his life had come to this.

She took a gulp of her wine and opened the book at Chapter One. Something started to nag at her.

CHAPTER THIRTY-ONE

Ensconced in her office, papers strewn across her desk, Julie Dunbar reached for her mug of tea. It had turned tepid, but was at least drinkable. She finished it off, grimacing when she'd drained the cup. A sharp rap on the door startled her. 'Yep. Come in,' she called. 'It's open.'

She half expected to see one of the residents, Bill probably, and was surprised to see that it was DS Winslet.

'Oh! Good morning! I'm sorry, I wasn't expecting you. Sorry for the mess, it's just . . . well, y'know.'

Winslet beamed a smile at her. 'Don't be daft. Should see the state of mine. Shocking's not the word for it. Too many case files piled up in the old in-tray. Yours looks like it's been done by that Marie Kondo woman compared to mine.'

Julie felt better about that, even though it was most likely an exaggeration. 'Well, thank you. What brings you back here today? I take it it's something to do with Dr Cooper, yes?' She caught DS Winslet's glance at the only empty chair in the office. 'Oh, I'm sorry! Please . . . sit down.'

Winslet nodded and parked herself on the chair. 'Actually, no. You've heard about the doctor, though, I take it?'

Julie rolled her eyes. 'Oh, yes. It's unbelievable. I . . . I'm so shocked. He seemed such a nice, genuine family man, y'know? He was always so patient and kind with the residents. His poor family must be beside themselves.'

'Yeah,' said DS Winslet. 'I've met the wife. She's devastated by it all. She claims to have had no idea and I actually believe her, having spent time with her. Nice lady.'

'You sound surprised. Do the wives usually cover for their husbands, then?'

DS Winslet's eyes widened and she nodded. 'Oh, yeah. Most of them go into shock first, then into denial and some . . . well, some just know that the old man's a wrong'un and just flat out lie for him. Sometimes, they're even involved. Look at Rose and Fred West.'

'Oh, yes. Of course. She knew about it all, didn't she? That was some years ago, wasn't it?'

'Hmm. And then there's those that have absolutely no idea and their entire world is destroyed in an instant. That's Mrs Cooper.'

The room fell silent for a moment as they both pondered how easy it was for people to deceive each other.

DS Winslet broke the silence. 'Reason I'm here is that, while we're still investigating Cooper, we've also had an allegation made about a care worker, Jackie Draper.'

Julie Dunbar was shocked. 'Draper?'

'Yeah. She does work here, yes?'

'Who made the allegation? Can I ask?'

'You can ask, but I can't tell you. You understand, I'm sure.'

'It was Bill, wasn't it?'

'I can't tell you that.'

'Bill. He hates her.'

'Hates her? Why?'

Julie sighed. 'Being honest, she's a Grade A bitch. A nasty piece of work who makes the residents' and some staff's lives a misery. Horrible woman.'

Winslet looked taken aback. 'I don't understand. If she's that bad, why do you employ her?'

Julie shrugged. 'You have no idea how short of staff we are in the care industry. It's an appalling state of affairs. Can't get people for love nor money. I have to keep her on until I can find a replacement and . . . I can't find one. Anywhere. Not many people want to work in this industry, I can tell you.'

'Wow,' said DS Winslet. 'I had no idea it was this bad.'

'Few people do. Only people who work in it. I have people come and go so fast it would make your head spin.' She felt sheepish all of a sudden. 'I'm sorry. This isn't your problem.'

'No. Not at all,' said DS Winslet. 'Don't feel bad about venting. It's good for us. Better out than in, eh?'

Julie gave her a smile. She liked Winslet.

'So, Bill . . . What's the problem between these two, then?' said Winslet.

Julie sighed. 'She goes out of her way to make his life a misery. She's always picking on him, verbally abusing him, and that's increased since she found out he was Old Bill — sorry, a police officer.'

Winslet waved away the remark. She'd heard a lot worse said about her profession, but that fact that Bill was a police officer was something new. 'A police officer? I didn't know that.'

'Oh, yes. Retired donkeys years ago. Apparently, he was quite high ranking and, from what I can see, quite famous.'

Winslet pulled her shoulders back and sat up. 'Was he, now?'

'Yes. He chased a serial killer back in the day. What did the press call him? Er . . . Jack. Jack something.'

'Not Jack the Ripper, was it?' Winslet said, with a wry smile.

'No,' Julie chuckled. 'You are naughty. He's not that old. Oh, who was it? The Knife! Yes, that's it . . . Jack the Knife. Never caught him. It still haunts him now.'

Susan tutted. 'Yeah, that's any detective's worst nightmare. They've all got one that got away, though. Guess this Jack was his. I'll bet it drives him crazy.'

'Oh, it does. He has a suitcase full of old press clippings and papers. Case papers, I think.'

Winslet held her hand up. 'I don't want to know that, thank you.'

Julie worried that she might have dropped Bill in it. 'Oh no! I'm sorry. Sorry. I didn't mean—'

Winslet shook her head. 'It's okay. Doesn't matter. Not important. I'm sure he got some sort of clearance to keep them. Copies probably. Why do you think he keeps them?'

'Don't know, really. Glory days, I suppose. Susan knows more about him. You could ask her. They're quite friendly.'

'Susan?'

'Susan Johnson. A really lovely girl. A good worker. Hard worker most of the time, but she has a tendency to spend a bit too much time talking with everyone. Not a bad thing, of course. It's nice, but she can overdo it. The residents and staff all love her — apart from Draper, of course.'

'Why doesn't Draper like her?'

'I don't really know. I can only think it's because Susan's well liked and she's not.'

'Sound like a charmer, this Draper woman.'

'That's one word for her.'

'Okay, well, I need to ask you a few questions about her. Is that all right?'

'Sure. I'll tell you what I know.'

'Thank you. I've done some digging and I understand that she lives in a council flat. Her husband, when he's around, is prone to giving her an alcohol-soaked beating from time to time. And that she has two teenage boys living at home with her. Both are well known to us — bit of burglary, drugs, theft. That sort of thing. So, from what I can see of it, they're . . . What's a nice way to say this? A bit of a troubled family, yes?'

Julie nodded.

'Can I ask . . . Have any of the residents mentioned credit cards or cash going missing? From their rooms, perhaps?'

She did have one or two reports of room theft made to her and she wrote them down, but no one actually said it

142

was Draper. They suspected as much, but never confirmed it. Her hands were tied without a firm allegation and she told Winslet.

'Do you still have copies of those reports? If you do, can I have them or copies of them, please?'

'Of course. I'll look for them in a minute.'

'What about drugs? You keep drugs here, right? For the care workers to administer, yes?'

Julie started to feel uneasy. 'Yes. Yes, we do. They're locked away in a cabinet. We have a medicine box for each resident. When we get their prescriptions, we put the medicines into each box and check them off against the resident's name. That way we know that their medicines are topped up. We also have a check sheet for when they're administered to a resident. We keep a daily eye on the drugs to make sure we don't run out. That could be a disaster in some cases.'

DS Winslet was nodding, interested. 'Okay, I see. And what sort of medicines do you keep?'

'Oh, God, all sorts. These people have so many ailments it would be easier to ask what we don't have.'

'Do you keep morphine here? Strong tranquilisers? That sort of thing.'

'Well, yes. Not lots of it, but yes to both. They're all on prescription, though.'

DS Winslet smiled. 'I know. I didn't think you were the El Chapo of old East London.'

Julie chuckled. She really did like Winslet.

'I take it this cabinet is secure at all times? I mean, apart from yourself, I presume, who else has access when you're not here? The night staff? All the care workers? That sort of thing.'

Julie stiffened. 'Oh. Oh . . . I see where you're going. You're asking if Draper has access?'

Winslet nodded slowly.

'Yes,' said Julie. 'The keys are kept in a lock box on the opposite wall to the cabinet.'

'And who has keys to that?'

'Everyone who works here.'

Winslet grimaced. 'So, not that secure, then? Could be a burglar's paradise, couldn't it?'

'I see what you mean. I suspect we're going to have to tighten that up, aren't we?'

'Oh, yes. Much tighter, I'm afraid. Tell you what, I can get a burglary squad officer to pop by and give you some advice. They'll be able to tell you the weak points of the building and stuff. You'll feel better once you've spoken to someone.'

Julie put her hand on her chest. 'Thank you, Grace. Oh, sorry. Can I call you Grace?'

'Of course. Not a problem. Look, do you know if any drugs have gone missing recently?'

Julie was taken aback. 'What? Not that I'm aware of. No.'

'Okay. That's good. Do me a favour, though. I appreciate you're busy but can you do me a quick inventory of what's in that cabinet and let me know if anything's missing?'

'Yes, of course. Does it have to be today? I am rather pushed. Meetings, I'm afraid.'

'No, doesn't have to be today. But as soon as you can, please. It's important.'

'I'll do it tomorrow. You don't think that Draper is involved in the deaths of the residents, do you? The drugs?'

'To be honest, I'm not sure. If anything is missing, then we'll have to dig into it a lot further.'

'Could she be in league with Dr Cooper?'

'In league? That's an expression I've not heard for years.'

Julie dropped her head slightly, embarrassed. 'Sorry. I read too many old crime novels, I suppose.'

DS Winslet chuckled. 'I'm teasing. Well, she could be. Could be she's nicking them for the two scrotes she calls sons. Could be that it's nothing to do with her at all, but I have to look into it.'

'Of course. I'll get onto it.'

DS Winslet got up from her chair and straightened her back. 'Thank you. I'm very grateful. Oh, two more things . .

. Can you keep what you're doing quiet? Don't want anyone knowing. And can you do it when Draper's off duty. Don't want her getting wind of it.'

'Of course.' Julie glanced at the paper calendar stuck to the wall with bits of Sellotape. 'Yep. She's off tomorrow, so that works nicely.'

They said their goodbyes, and Julie watched as DS Winslet let herself out of the building. She stopped on the top step, looked to her left and saw Bill looking back at her, smiling. She smiled back, gave him a little wave and walked down the steps.

CHAPTER THIRTY-TWO

By the time DS Grace Winslet got back to the station, it had started to rain. She got out of her car, locked it up, and headed for the back door to the building just as the skies ruptured, unleashing an unexpected and relentless deluge with a magnitude akin to that of a biblical flood. Caught in the open and completely exposed to the elements, she sprinted frantically towards the door and then struggled to press the buttons on the number keypad for a few seconds before the door opened and gave her sanctuary.

Once inside, she stood on a coconut-fibre carpet and shook out her arms, sending rivulets of water droplets across the floor. She rubbed water off her face with both hands and pushed her hair back tight against her head to keep her face dry.

'Morning, Grace. Is it raining out?' Her friend Lisa, a uniformed officer, was in a chirpy mood this morning. Lisa stepped past her and pushed her face up against the glass square in the door and looked out into the yard.

'Nope,' said Grace. 'I'm pioneering fully clothed indoor showering. I'm hoping it'll catch on and make me a fortune.'

Lisa smiled at her. 'Fortunes are not for you, babe. You love this bloody job too much.'

'Do I?'

'You know you do.'

'Hmm. Sometimes.'

'Having a bad day?'

'I wasn't until just now. I'm saturated.'

'Why didn't you sit in your car and wait? I would have done.'

Grace gave her a look. 'D'you know? I never thought of that. What a tit!'

Lisa chuckled. 'It's stopping now.'

Grace sniffed. 'Wonderful. I'll wait until the sun comes out and go and stand in that for an hour or so. Should dry out nicely. Look, gotta go. Something's cropped up and I need to talk to Carter about it. If you're about this evening, d'you want to go and grab a drink, about eight?' She started up the stairs.

'Ooh, sorry, babe! I've got a date tonight.'

'Blind?'

'Don't know. It didn't say anything about that on his profile. I expect I'll find out when I get there. Best I take some treats for his dog.'

'Idiot! You know what I mean. Be careful. Text me where you're going.'

'Will do. And, speaking of being careful, you too.'

Grace was puzzled. 'What d'you mean?'

Lisa nodded at Grace's chest. She looked down. Her blouse was wet and the thin fabric made a point of showing her nipples. She pulled her jacket across her chest. 'Oh, Christ!'

'Yep. That'll do nothing to quieten the boys down, will it?'

Holding her jacket tight across her body, Grace walked off up the stairs. 'Don't forget . . . text me!'

After a five-minute stop in the ladies changing room, Grace had managed to towel dry her hair with an old T-shirt she had. She ran a brush through it and felt a bit better. The blouse was going to be the problem. No one else was about so she couldn't even ask someone if she could borrow a top from them. A sweatshirt would have been useful at this point.

She sighed and walked out.

* * *

DCI Carter was going through his plans for the day when DS Winslet knocked on his door. The national press was onto the Cooper case by now and he had a press conference at noon. They smelled blood in the water and Carter had to feed them. Better to give them a few little titbits than let them feed themselves. Cooper was out on bail and had bolted with his wife to their house in the country. The press would find him. They always did.

'Come in!' Carter shouted without looking up.

Winslet walked in and stood in the doorway. 'Don't say a word, guv.'

Carter lifted his head. 'Oh. Did you get caught in that lot?'

She glared at him silently for a moment. 'Just a bit.'

'Yes, I can see.' He nodded at her chest.

'Yeah, well. Try not to. Can I sit down?'

'Yeah, of course. Take a pew.'

She pulled her jacket tighter, sat herself down and wriggled around a bit on the chair, uncomfortable in her wet trousers. 'I've just been back to the home and had a chat with that Mrs Dunbar. Nice lady.'

Carter sipped at his tea. Winslet eyed it enviously.

'Sorry, Grace. You want one?'

'That'd be nice. Please.'

'Okay.' He waggled his cup at her. 'Go and make yourself one and I'll have another one too, please.'

Winslet, for obvious reasons, wasn't going outside just yet. 'Yeah. No. I'll get you one in a minute. I found out something interesting while talking to her.'

'Talking to who?'

'Tch. To Mrs Dunbar.'

'Oh, yeah. What's that, then?'

'Turns out our friend Bill Roach used to be a copper.'

Carter was surprised. 'Yeah? When?'

'I'm not sure. I think it was years ago. Many, years ago. He was a DCI too, by all accounts.'

'That must have been back when coppers were coppers and not the bloody social-working, pen-pushing office wallahs we are today.'

'I'm just wondering why he never mentioned it.'

'Why would he?'

Winslet shrugged. 'It's just that every old copper I've ever known likes to talk about "the good old days", don't they?'

'Yeah, I suppose. To be fair, though, he did put us on to Cooper. So, good on him. Still got his head in the game even though everything else is shot to pieces.' He chuckled to himself.

'Yeah, he did. Can't fault him for observation. I'm just surprised, that's all.'

'Anything else come out of this meeting?'

'A few bits. I went down there to get some info on this Draper woman who works there. Bill told us she's his number two suspect. Remember?'

Carter shook his head and shrugged. 'He did?'

'Oh, for Christ's sake, guv. I told you this on the phone.'

Carter gave her a mischievous grin. 'You're right. You did. I remember it well, now you mention it. And? Anything?'

'Yep. Seems she's a nasty bitch who hates the world and everyone in it. She makes resident's and staff's life hell, according to Dunbar.'

'I thought she was supposed to be a carer? Doesn't sound like she's up to the job.'

'She's not. But the industry is so undermanned, it's crazy. I think they'd take on Myra Hindley, they're so desperate for people.'

Carter grinned. 'They'll have a job. She's long dead now and good riddance to her.'

'Anyway, I found out that pretty much everyone who works there has access to the drugs cabinet.'

Carter just shook his head.

'I know. Crazy, right? Anyway, I've asked her to do a full inventory of the cabinet they're kept in and, with a bit of luck, I'll have it tomorrow or the day after. I've also asked her to check some reports she has about property going missing from residents' bedrooms. I want to see if it matches up with her starting work there. It's a step.'

'Okay, back up. Are you now thinking this Draper woman could be involved somehow?'

'Don't know. Could be. She has motive. Abusive home life, her two teenagers are on the rob and, of course, they do drugs. Must be like a sweetie shop for her.'

'Fair point. Any history of violence from her? Anything that might suggest she'd throw in with Cooper?'

Winslet pulled a face. 'I did a check on the way back here. She's got a bit of previous. Mostly drunk and disorderly. Couple of pub fights. Bit of ABH. Nothing outrageous. Low level, really. Handling stolen goods from her son's burglaries. Again, nothing spectacular and nothing that would shed light on her working with Cooper. If anything, I just fancy her for nicking from people's rooms.'

'Well, I've still not ruled out Cooper yet. My money's on him alone.'

'Why? Something happened?'

'In his interview, I told Cooper that I knew what was on his laptop to put the shits up him — see if he'd cough to something. But I know why he didn't want us snooping around at his home. Just got a report back from the forensic computer boys. They've had a field day with his PC and laptop.'

Winslet sat forward. 'Go on.'

'In total, one thousand, six hundred and eighty-seven images of kiddie porn.'

Winslet's jaw dropped. 'Oh, Christ!'

'Yep. Oh, Christ indeed.'

She sucked in a deep breath before releasing it. 'I never had him down for that. Christ, his poor wife! She'll have a heart attack when she finds out. That's awful.'

'I know. I'm going to charge him with that at some point. But wait . . . there's more, as the Americans say. Do you know what gerontophilia is?'

Winslet shook her head.

'Glad to hear it. In its basic form, it's sexual attraction toward the elderly.'

'What?'

'Wrinklies. Much older. Much, much older. The third age, old.'

'No!'

'Yep. Cooper also had a load of nudey pictures of old women on there too.'

'So, he's . . .'

'Both ends of the scale. Young and old.'

'Were there any videos of the old people?'

He shuddered. 'Nope. I would imagine it's a bit difficult to make sex videos if you've got dodgy knees, a dodgy back, hip replacements and no teeth.'

'I suppose.'

'Anyway, the magistrate ordered the surrender of his passport before giving him bail, so he's gone to his country pile with the missus to escape the press. Vultures are after him now, big time. I'm briefing them at twelve.'

'So, if he's got a thing for the most vulnerable members of society. Kiddies and oldies. Nasty man. A very nasty man.'

CHAPTER THIRTY-THREE

Grace Winslet said goodbye to everybody in the office and was about to knock off for the day when her phone rang. She tutted and looked at the screen: *DUNBAR*. She hesitated a second or two before answering.

'Hello, Mrs Dunbar. How are you? Didn't expect to hear from you today.'

'I know, but I need to talk to you.' Her voice sounded a bit tinny.

'Is it important? I was just about to pack up for the day.'

'I'm afraid it is. Some things are missing.'

'Things?'

'Drugs.'

'I'm on my way.' Grace hung up and sighed. She'd been looking forward to a sensible knock-off time with hopefully an early night — a bit of shopping on the way home, TV in her pyjamas and bed. A real slob-out night. It was not to be.

She popped her head around Carter's door. He was always first in and last out. 'Guv?'

'Hmm?' He was shuffling papers around on his desk.

'Just had a call from Mrs Dunbar. Reckons some drugs have gone AWOL from the cabinet. I'm going to swing past there on my way home.'

'Want me to come with you?'

She shook her head. 'No point. I'll go and chat with her and see what's up first.'

'Okay. Be careful. If you need anything, give me a call.'

Grace smiled. She knew he would turn out if she made the call. That was one of the things she most admired about Harry Carter: not one to shirk or pass responsibility. He was always there for his team and would back them to the hilt if it was necessary.

'Will do, boss. You have a good night.'

He waved at her as she closed the door.

* * *

At Crown Woods, Grace Winslet was greeted by a smiling, fresh-faced young woman who was presumably a carer working the late shift.

'Evening,' she said. 'Can I help you?'

'Hi, I'm DS Winslet. I've had a call from Mrs Dunbar. She asked me to pop in and see her.' Grace pulled her warrant card out of her bag and showed it to the woman. After a cursory look at it, she stood aside and let her in.

The carer introduced herself politely as Gemma Kent and then led Grace into the reception area. 'She won't be long. She's got herself caught up with one of the residents. Another one refusing her medication. Happens a lot.'

Grace's heart sank. Another delay before getting home.

'You're welcome to wait in the lounge area or the kitchen,' said Gemma. 'She shouldn't be too long. Would you like a cup of tea? Coffee, maybe?'

'Tea would be nice, please. Milk, no sugar. Thanks.'

'Where will you be?'

'If you're going to the kitchen, I might as well come with you.'

As they headed to the kitchen, Winslet had a quick glance around the place. The home itself was an old Victorian mansion, huge by any standards. Grace had googled what she could about the place and discovered that the man who owned it originally had left it in his will for the benefit of the sick and elderly. She presumed it was his portrait hanging in the lobby, of a pleasant-looking man in his sixties with a round face, red cheeks and a pair of lips that were now locked for ever in the sort of pout that would put any Instagrammer to shame.

There was a collection of head-and-shoulder photographs of the current members of staff with their names underneath. She stopped to look. There was Mrs Dunbar, Gemma, Susan Johnson — a pretty girl, Grace thought — Nadine Aquino, Lea Salonga, Aya Awosika, Stefan Banach — the only man she could see in the line-up — Jenny Teach and one Jacqueline Draper. The rumours were true: a hard-faced bitch to be sure. There were a few other faces, all women, making up four more carers, a few admin staff and the cook, but she'd seen who she needed to.

She walked into the kitchen, saw Gemma fiddling with a bright yellow mug and felt her heart sink a bit when she saw Bill sitting at the table with one of his mates.

Bill looked up and waved his bony hand at her. 'Hello, Grace,' he said, cheerily. 'What're you doing here? Did you miss me?'

Grace forced her broadest smile. 'You guessed it, Bill. Couldn't stay away from you.'

Bill's mate scoffed. 'You can have him, love. He drives me mental. Who are you then, sweetheart?'

Grace cocked her head. 'Sorry, I'm Detective Sergeant Winslet. Grace Winslet.' She walked over to offer her hand. 'And you are?'

The old man stood up and took it. Old school. 'Name's Charlie.' He nodded toward Bill. 'I'm banged up here for me sins along with the likes of this old sod.'

'Nice to meet you, Charlie.'

Gemma handed her the yellow mug now full of hot tea.

'Siddown, love,' said Charlie. 'Come and join the old codgers club. Sadly, there's less and less of us each month.'

Charlie seemed alright. 'Yeah, why not?' she said, as he pulled out a chair for her.

'What brings you back to us, Grace?' said Bill.

'Just looking into a few things still,' she said.

'Something to do with Dr Cooper?' Bill asked.

'Hmm. But you know I can't tell you what, Bill, so don't ask me, you crafty old sod.'

The remark caught Bill by surprise. 'What d'you mean?'

'You know.'

Bill looked puzzled.

'You. How come you never mentioned you were ex-job?'

It was Charlie's turn to look surprised. 'Didn't he? Blimey! That's unusual. He never stops banging on about it to anyone who stands still long enough. Ain't that right, mate?' He winked at an embarrassed Bill.

'I'm sorry, love,' said Bill. 'Didn't see the need. Plus, if I had, you might have thought I was just some old-fart copper trying to make myself busy and big myself up. I needed you to look at me as just a resident and not as an old DCI.'

'Maybe,' she said. 'But I would have preferred the info to have come from you as an ex-copper, Bill. At least you know what you're looking for so I would have given you more credence. And, if no one's said it to you yet, nice catch on the pattern of resident deaths to Cooper's attendance.'

'That why you're here, Grace?' said Charlie. 'To blow smoke up his arse? Please don't do that. He'll be a right pain if you've come to congratulate him. Won't be able to stop going on about it, I promise yer.'

She chuckled. 'No. I'm here just as a follow-up. I'm after a few bits of paper that Mrs Dunbar might have and I popped in on the off-chance on my way home. She's busy, though. That's why you've been blessed with my company.'

'I'm good with that,' said Charlie. 'Let's hope she goes home and forgets about you. You can stay here all night.' A cheeky grin spread across his face.

Grace treated him to a sideways glance. 'Down, boy.'

Charlie put on a sad face. 'Sadly, that's the state of play these days, sweetheart. God bless old age, eh?' He laughed at his own joke and nudged Bill on the arm.

Mrs Dunbar popped her head around the door. 'Grace!' she called. 'I'll be two minutes. Bill, would you mind staying for a chat, too?'

Bill frowned. 'Okay.'

Mrs Dunbar looked at Charlie.

'Right,' Charlie said. 'Got it. Civvy's not wanted. I'll be in the lounge when you're done, Gracie love. Come and say goodbye, eh?' Charlie heaved himself up and looked at her expectantly.

'Tell you what,' she said. 'Let me have your room number and I'll come and tuck you in when I'm done.' She raised her eyebrows quickly.

Charlie stared at her. 'What?'

She smiled at him, more a grin really.

'Oh, you're a saucy one. Shouldn't tease an old man like that. Me blood pressure just went through the roof. I think I need me statins.' He walked off chuckling to himself and waved once.

CHAPTER THIRTY-FOUR

After Charlie had left the room, Mrs Dunbar poured herself a cup of tea and sat down with Grace and Bill. 'I'm sorry I kept you waiting, Grace. Bit of a crisis with one of the residents. All sorted out now.'

Grace shrugged. 'That's okay. Stuff happens. Not a problem.'

Mrs Dunbar looked around her to make sure no one was within earshot.

'Should we do this in your office?' said Grace. 'You look a bit concerned.'

'No, no. Not at all. I'm glad to be out of that place, to be honest. I just wanted to sit and have a cup of tea somewhere else. Change of scenery. I'm fine.'

'Okay then,' said Grace. 'What do you have?'

'Bill,' said Mrs Dunbar, 'everything we say here is to be kept quiet. *Very* quiet. You understand? No gossiping with Charlie, alright?'

Bill nodded. 'Okay. What's up?'

'I did as you asked, Grace. I checked over the inventory for the drugs cabinet. Some things are missing.'

Grace sighed. Bill looked confused.

'What's going on?' he said. 'What's been happening?'

Cradling her mug in two hands, Mrs Dunbar looked across the table at him. 'Grace had a few questions about Draper. She asked me to carry out an inventory of the drug cabinet, which I did.'

'Hang on. You think Draper's nicking drugs?'

'I asked the question, Bill,' said Grace. 'Just wondering if she could have been involved with the doctor. Not saying she was, just wondering, that's all.'

'Well, I said she was a nasty piece of work. Nothing she does surprises me. Not even a spot of cold-blooded murder.'

'We'll see,' said Grace. 'Go on, Mrs Dunbar. What'd you find out?'

Mrs Dunbar looked up at the ceiling briefly before looking straight at Grace. 'Okay, no beating around. I've lost two bottles of morphine. They're on the sheet but not in the cabinet.'

'Oh, crap!' said Bill. 'That's not good.'

Grace closed her eyes for a second. 'Okay. When was the last time a check was carried out?'

'About two weeks ago?'

'About?'

'Sorry. Yes. Two weeks ago.'

'And how often is a check carried out?'

'Every two weeks. So that's all normal.'

'Two weeks? I would have thought every day would be more appropriate,' said Grace.

Mrs Dunbar looked sheepish. 'Yeah, I know. I agree. It should be, but it's one of those things that gets overlooked when we're busy. And we're always busy.'

'I'm not having a dig,' said Grace. 'It's just an observation. But really?'

Mrs Dunbar smiled weakly. She obviously knew she'd made a mistake with the storage and handling of drugs. 'I'll get on top of it. Soon.'

'Is Draper in work today?' Grace asked.

'No. Day off.'

'Okay. Have you searched her locker yet?'

Mrs Dunbar shook her head vigorously. 'What? No. Thought we could do it together. Y'know . . . witnesses and everything. Shall we do it now?'

'Do you have the power to do it,' asked Grace, 'or do I need a warrant?'

'No, you don't. I've double-checked the company policy. It says that senior management have the right to check a member of staff's belongings, and that includes their locker spaces, for items that may have been stolen from the home. Words to that effect anyway.'

'Good enough for me. But I'll make a note in my notebook and ask that you sign it as giving me permission to search her locker. Keeps it all neat and tidy down the road.'

Draper's locker was in the basement area of the building and the three made their way down in the lift. Bill couldn't have managed the stairs. Once the doors opened it was a short walk along a narrow corridor letting into a reasonably sized area with ten double lockers lined up neatly.

'Hers is this one here.' Mrs Dunbar pointed to a grey, manky-looking locker at the back of the little room. 'The one with the devil sticker on it.'

'Seems only right,' Bill muttered.

Grace examined the padlock. It was secure, but the lock itself was nothing special. Standard. Mrs Dunbar fumbled in her jacket and pulled out a small bunch of locker keys. After trying a few of them, she had success on the fourth attempt. She pulled open the door and the three peered inside.

The top shelf had a couple of battered, dog-eared novels, both Martina Cole. There was a notebook, a couple of pens, a small mirror, an open box of tissues and a makeup bag. Grace pulled on a pair of white latex gloves, took out the bag, opened it up and rifled through the contents. There was nothing you wouldn't expect to find.

The lower section was used to hang clothes and store boots and bags. An old jacket was hanging up. Grace checked the pockets: empty, save for a few used tissues. She knelt down and pulled out a weathered rucksack that that lay crumpled on top of a pair of ankle-length boots. Inside the bag was a half-empty water bottle, a packet of crisps and a bar of fruit-and-nut chocolate. Draper had had a few squares. There was an old creased-up T-shirt bearing the slogan *Born to Be Bad*. Bill raised his eyes and shook his head when he saw it.

Grace pulled out the boots. They were plastic made to look like leather and were old and tatty. There were scuff marks on both and the heels were worn down. Draper clearly walked on the outside of her feet. Grace looked up at Mrs Dunbar. 'These feel a bit heavy.' She squeezed the side of the boot. There was no give. Something solid was inside. She reached in and pulled out a bottle. She held it up to Mrs Dunbar and Bill. 'Well, there's your morphine.' She picked up the other boot and repeated her actions. 'And here's Contestant Number Two. Both bottles, Mrs Dunbar.'

Mrs Dunbar rubbed her eyes. 'Okay. She'll have to go.'

Grace stood up. 'Yep, but I'm going to have to nick her first. What's your procedure for this sort of thing?'

'Well, first thing is, I have to let her know we carried out a search and what we found. Then I'll verbally inform her that she's terminated with immediate effect, followed by a written letter of confirmation.'

Grace felt uneasy. 'I think that'll cause a few problems. I'm thinking that she'll start screaming that she was fitted up. Bill, she might even say that you planted it, seeing as how you hate each other.'

'Me! I don't know nothing about it. I just came down here with you two.'

'I know, I know. But you know what these people are like. She's not gonna hold her hands up, is she? No, she'll scream blue murder about it.'

'So, what do you suggest?' said Mrs Dunbar.

Grace sighed. 'Well, I've got an idea, but you might not like it. For now, though, I suggest we lock it up again and, if anyone asks, we were never here.'

CHAPTER THIRTY-FIVE

At 9.30 a.m. the following morning, Winslet, DCI Carter and a third member of the team, DC Alwyn Thomas, arrived at the Crown Woods Retirement Home. At 9.40 a.m. Mrs Dunbar called in all the staff that were then on duty. Jackie Draper, Susan Johnson, Gemma Kent and Lee Truby were all called into the office at the same time.

With the four members of staff, three police officers and Mrs Dunbar, the office was at bursting point. There was nowhere else to go that didn't have residents milling around, and what Mrs Dunbar had to say was not for public ears.

'I'm sorry I pulled you all away from your duties,' she said. 'But I'm afraid it's a rather delicate matter. These three people are police officers and they are here at my request.' The members of staff all looked a little wary of what was happening.

'Yesterday, I carried out an inventory of the drugs cabinet and I found that two bottles of morphine had gone missing. Now, as much as I really don't like to do this, policy tells me that I must call in the police and, in their presence, I must carry out a search of all the lockers.'

Draper scoffed. 'You're not looking in mine.'

'Excuse me?' said Mrs Dunbar. Everyone turned to face her.

Draper's body language changed in an instant. She became confrontational. Old habits when in the face of authority.

'I said *you're not looking in mine*. Unless someone here's got a warrant.'

'I'm not sure you understand how this works, Miss . . . Draper, is it?' said DCI Carter. 'We don't need a warrant for this, love. We've been invited in and given full permission from the manager of this premises to carry out a search for controlled drugs, and that's exactly what we're going to do.'

'In that case, *love*, you crack on. Just not with mine, okay?'

'I'm beginning to think you may have something to hide, *love*,' said Carter. 'You seem to be a bit defensive about this. Innocent people don't usually have an issue. Are you innocent?'

Draper eyed him up and down as if she'd met his type of copper before: all dressed in his best suit, collar and tie, fancying himself as the next Sherlock Holmes, bigging it up in front of everyone, flash.

'Yep. I am innocent and I know my rights.'

'Of course you do,' said Grace. 'Why wouldn't you with your two boys in and out of the nick every other day. Should think you do know your rights. Except, it turns out you don't, do you? We wouldn't be here if we didn't know what we were doing. So, you might want to get a refund on the law course you must have taken online.'

'Oi, bitch! Don't you go bad-mouthing my two boys. You don't get to talk about them, understood?'

Grace gave her a huge grin. 'Oops. Too late. Just did.'

Draper moved forward, fast. DC Thomas grabbed her by the collar and pulled her back as Grace readied herself. Mrs Dunbar was looking very worried. She clearly had no desire to be caught up in the middle of what was brewing.

Draper struggled to get DC Thomas to let go. She whirled around and started to slap at his face. He put his arms up and backed away from the sudden assault. Grace moved. She grabbed Draper by the head, pulled her away from Thomas and slammed her, belly first, onto Mrs Dunbar's desk. Draper struggled furiously and swore like a trooper before DCI Carter slapped on a pair of handcuffs and straightened her up.

'DC Thomas,' he said.

The officer looked at him.

'All yours.'

DC Thomas nodded. 'Jackie Draper. You're under arrest for assault on police — namely, me. You do not have to say anything. But it may harm your defence if you do not mention when questioned something which you later rely on in court. Anything you do say may be given in evidence.'

'You're all filth!'

'Some of us are quite lovely,' said Grace. 'You just need to get to know us better.'

'I'll do you, you cocky bitch. Think you're funny, do you? I'll show funny when I get out of these handcuffs.'

'Okay, Draper,' said Carter. 'Enough of the silly games. We're going down to the lockers to do what we came here to do. You're coming too.'

Visibly shaken by the altercation, Mrs Dunbar told the other members of staff to wait in the office and to leave only in an emergency.

* * *

Mrs Dunbar undid the lock on Draper's locker. If looks had heat, Draper's hard stare would have cooked her from the inside out. Everybody but Grace backed away as she started her search from the top. A few things had been moved, presumably by Draper when she came on duty, but otherwise all the same things were there.

All for show, Grace patted down the coat, dug into the pockets and, finding nothing, moved down to the boots. She took out one and then the other. 'These feel a bit heavy.'

Draper scowled as Grace pulled out a bottle of morphine. 'What? That's not mine. I never put that there! This is a bloody fit-up!' DC Thomas held her arm a bit tighter. She jerked her arm away, but he held on.

163

Grace ignored her and pulled the second bottle from the other boot.

'Oh, come on! You're bloody well joking! I ain't nicked them. Why would I do that? No good to me.'

Grace stood up and raised one of the bottles. She squinted as she read the label. 'Maybe not you, but both your boys have a bit of a drug problem, don't they?'

Draper sneered at her. 'That's it. I'm saying nothing until I get a solicitor. You scumbags must have planted it.'

'Don't see how,' said Carter. 'You were here the whole time. You saw us find it and I'm pretty sure one of us would've noticed her slip two bottles of morphine out of her sleeve and drop them in your boots. Think we all would. DC Thomas, do the honours, please.'

DC Thomas nodded. 'Jackie Draper, I'm also arresting you on suspicion of being in possession of a controlled substance with intent to supply.' He cautioned her again.

'Leave off,' she said. 'I've got nothing to say. Get me a brief.'

'In good time, Mrs Draper,' Carter said. 'First, though, we're going to swing past your house and do a little search of the place.'

At that, Draper totally lost any semblance of control. She ranted and raved as she was dragged up the stairs and out into the street. Pedestrians gawked as they passed her by, shocked by her railing against the unfairness of it all. Nothing could stop her as she yelled and cursed, her voice echoing off the facades of the imposing buildings that surrounded her. Kicking and screaming, she was bundled into the back of Carter's car and continued to scream and yell obscenities until they were out of sight.

CHAPTER THIRTY-SIX

Jackie Draper's neighbours were not unused to seeing her in trouble. She was the nightmare neighbour next door and spent most of her days causing problems and verbally abusing anyone who said anything against her or her sons. Many of them had heard her and her wayward husband fighting and all of them turned a deaf ear when it came to reporting it. Nobody wanted to get involved with this lot. Her closest friend, Vicky Shorne, four doors down, couldn't convince her to leave him, even after his last assault on her a year ago had left her black and blue. His affairs with some of the local women made no difference either.

For some reason, her actions gave people the impression that the sun shone out of his backside and she would say or do nothing against him. Her oldest son, Colin, once got in the way of of his drunken rages and, for his trouble, received four stitches to his forehead and a severely bruised and swollen lip.

Her old man was no good, a loser, but she loved him and that was that. Through thick and thin.

As she climbed out of Carter's car, still handcuffed, her husband, awake surprisingly early, was watching out of the kitchen window. He was not happy. He wrenched open the street door as Jackie, flanked by the coppers, approached along the path. He came screaming towards them waving a hammer in his hand.

'Darren! No!' Jackie Draper screamed at him.

* * *

Grace and Carter let go of Jackie Draper quickly and moved away from her.

'Oi!' Carter shouted at her husband. 'Put it down! Now!'

Grace pulled out her phone. She knew this wasn't going to suddenly quieten down. Darren Draper was too wound up. His face was a bright red colour and the look on his face said *murder*.

DC Thomas stood his ground. A young, fit rugby player built like a bull, he'd had more than his share of fights since becoming a police officer. He probably didn't fancy his attacker for much, and before he took another four steps, Thomas most likely had lined up six possible ways to subdue him.

'Darren! Darren! Don't! Don't be stupid!' Jackie Draper was raging again, no doubt sure in the knowledge that Darren was going to get himself nicked and, with waving a hammer about, probably given a good hiding once they had him. And she'd know they'd get him eventually. 'Go indoors! Go in! It's alright! It's okay!'

If Darren Draper was the sort of man who rarely listened to his wife then today wasn't going to be an exception. Rage and drink combined had shot out the last few brain cells he had that dealt with reason.

DC Thomas prepared himself and planted himself sideways on.

'Oh, yeah?' Darren shouted. 'You bloody want some, do yer? Have some of this then, copper!' He raised the hammer over his head, and as he started to swing it downward, Carter, who had side-stepped to end up behind him, grabbed Darren by the hair and yanked him downward. As he lost his footing and began to tumble backward, Carter dropped his fist down sledgehammer hard, straight onto Darren's nose. He dropped like a stone, out for the count. Carter stood over Darren's sprawled-out body, his face a mass of red from the explosion of blood from his nose. 'Bad boy!' he said.

Jackie Draper went ballistic at seeing her old man bite the dust. 'You bastard! Why'd you do that?'

Carter looked up at her. 'Really? You can't work that out?' He shook his head.

DC Thomas picked up the hammer and put it inside his jacket. He knelt down, rolled Darren onto his front, and applied a set of handcuffs. Before he stood up, he turned Darren's face onto its side and pulled his jaw down to ensure he could breathe.

'Guv,' Grace said, 'I've got some backup coming. Area car and the van are both nearby. Wasn't expecting all this to kick off. Want me to cancel them?'

Carter smiled. 'No, no. Keep 'em coming. They can take the old man away for us. She can go in the van when we're done having a poke around the house.'

'I'll have you copper. I swear I will!' Draper screamed at him.

Carter ignored her. 'Okay. In we go, then. Time for a look around.'

They stepped inside the hall and were hit by the smell, a mixture of wet dog and filth. There was beer in the mix too. Lots of it. The fetid stench of urine topped it off. Ahead of them, the kitchen door was open. A waste bin overflowed in the corner, filled mostly with pizza boxes and beer bottles. They wandered deeper into the house. The wallpaper was covered with half a dozen layers of emulsion, which did nothing to hide the years of grime and dirt. Smoke filled the air and obscured most of the light from the windows. A television droned in the corner and a half-empty bottle of whisky sat on the floor along with a glass.

'Jackie,' said Carter, 'did you give the cleaner the day off again?'

'You're a funny git, copper. Won't be making jokes when I get out of these cuffs and bite your bloody face off. See if I don't.'

'How pleasant. But that's okay. I'm up to date with my tetanus jab.'

DC Thomas walked into the room. 'Locals have arrived. They're dealing with the old man for me.'

'Excellent,' said Carter. Do me a favour and stay in the kitchen with her for a minute while me and Grace have a look around.' He looked at the surly figure of Draper, staring at him with impotent rage.

A uniformed police officer popped his head around the street door. 'Hello, guv. I see someone's been busy in the garden.'

'Hmm,' said Carter. 'Seems he's not a friend of the police. Poor chap fell over.'

'Where'd you want him taken? Hospital or nick?'

'Is he breathing?'

'I think so. I tested him with my shoe on the way in and he grunted, so, yeah, he's alive.'

'To the nick, then. Can you do me a favour? Book him in and bin him up for me and tell the custody sergeant I'll be there within the hour.'

'Course. See you later.'

* * *

One hour and twenty minutes later, Carter, Winslet and Thomas were back at the station, having found nothing of note at the Drapers' property beyond a few bits of burned tinfoil, the odd syringe and a couple of unopened iPad Pros that would need to be answered for. There was certainly nothing that would help in relation to Jackie Draper's theft of morphine. Carter told the custody sergeant that he would interview her in an hour and Darren straight after. In the meantime, he was going up to his office to have a cup of tea and make a few notes.

Carter plonked himself down in his office chair and swung his feet up on the desk. In his hand was tea, made by another member of his team. He rubbed his face a few times before sighing and taking a sip.

Winslet sat opposite him. Coffee for her. 'That was a bit of a blowout, wasn't it?' she said.

Carter nodded. 'Thought we might have got a bit more to sink our teeth into.'

'Hmm. Still, we've got her on theft of a controlled substance, obstruction and assault on police, so we can see what the interview brings up.'

'Still think she's got anything to do with Dr Cooper?'

'I really don't know. I doubt it, but she's such a nasty cow, maybe she had something on him. Maybe she caught him in the act and blackmailed him. Maybe he gives her drugs as well.'

'So, we don't fancy her for killing the wrinkly people?'

She sighed loudly. 'No. She's a violent bitch. Nasty. But injecting people? No. Not her game. I get the impression she'd rather hound them to their graves over a long period of time. More her style.'

Carter's officer door suddenly flew inward. Holding the door handle was DC Coral Sparks. 'Guv, you need to see this. Shit's hit the fan!'

He was up on his feet before Sparks had stepped back out into the main office. He reached the door in moments. His squad of detectives were all crowded around in a semi-circle, looking at the TV screen on the wall.

'What's happened?' Carter said.

'It's Cooper,' said Sparks. 'Bugger's gone and done himself in!'

Winslet closed her eyes, hung her head and sighed loudly.

CHAPTER THIRTY-SEVEN

'Morning all,' said Bill, as he tottered into the kitchen. 'Any tea on the go?'

'In your mug, Bill,' said Susan. 'Already on the table.'

He touched his forelock as a way of thanks and made his way over to the table where he sat himself down next to Charlie. Charlie looked up and gave him a thin grin.

'Alright, Bill?' he said.

'Yeah. Not bad. Usual bloody aches and pains. You?'

'Not bad. Every day above ground's a win for me, eh?'

Bill chuckled. 'It's quiet in here this morning. Where is everybody?'

'Watching the telly.'

'Unusual for this time of the day. Something happened in the world?' Bill picked up his tea. His hand shook, causing him to spill a little.

'Yep.'

Bill took out his medicine kit from his dressing gown pocket and placed it on the table. He pushed it forward with one of his bony fingers. 'What's happened, then?'

Charlie shook his head. 'You not watch the box last night?'

Bill shook his head. 'No. Went to bed about nine. Tired out.'

'Turns out our Dr Cooper topped himself.'

'What? He's killed himself? No? When?'

'His missus found him yesterday when she got in. They're saying suicide but not saying how he did it.'

'Did they say *why* he did it?'

'First thing I thought was it was guilt from killing people in here. But it turns out your lot found a ton of dirty kiddie pics on his computers.'

'Oh, Jesus!'

'It's so sad,' said Susan. 'All the people who have been hurt by him. Probably couldn't handle the shame.'

'Sad?' said Bill. 'What's sad about a bloke who gets off on that sort of thing killing himself? Good bloody riddance to him, I say.'

Charlie nodded. 'You always said he was a wrong'un and you were bloody right. Sorry I wound you up about it, Bill. I take me hat off to yer.'

Bill blew into his mug. 'It's alright, mate. I know you didn't mean anything by it. Has the news said anything more about the murders in here?'

'They're just saying that the police haven't ruled him out and that their enquiries are still ongoing,' said Susan.

'Well, I feel for his missus and kids, if he had any,' said Bill, 'but he's no loss to society as far as I'm concerned.' He finally took a sip of his tea.

'What if you're wrong about him killing people?' said Susan.

Bill shrugged. 'I doubt I am. But even if I was, I'll bet there's more to this child pornography than meets the eye. It's a bit extreme to do himself in, even if he did have loads of pictures.'

'Could be shame, Bill. Some people just can't take it.'

'Could be he was more involved than we know,' said Bill. 'Could be he took the photos. Could be he was *in* the photos.

171

Could be he was in with a group of abusers. You read about that sort of thing all the time. Could be lots of reasons why he did it and we won't know until the facts come out. And until they do, I'm sticking with good riddance to him. If I'm wrong about him, then that means I'll have to put my detective hat back on and start digging around again because *someone's* bloody killed them, haven't they?'

'Oh! More good news for you two . . .' said Susan. 'Did you hear Draper got arrested yesterday?'

'What?' Both men said it at the same time, although Bill knew exactly what was going on.

'Yeah. Found two bottles of morphine in her locker. She went mad and had to be dragged out, kicking and screaming. She tried to attack DS Winslet and that didn't end too well for her. So, we're going to be even more short-staffed.'

'Bloody hell!' said Charlie. 'This place is a right hotbed of crime. So, what happens to her now?'

Susan shrugged. 'Well, there's no mucking about. That's instant dismissal.'

'What about her things in here, her locker?' said Charlie.

She shrugged again. 'I don't know. They may be couriered back to her or she may have to come and get them. Knowing her, she'll be brazen enough to come back in and collect them. Once last sneer at everybody. Best you stay out of the way, Bill.'

'Why? What have I done?'

'She knows you hate her,' said Charlie. 'She hates you. Probably thinks you called the coppers on her. Got her nicked. Whatever she thinks, best keep yer nut down. Don't give her a chance to go off on one.'

Bill put his mug down and reached for the digestives. 'Oh, I'll be ready for her, don't you worry. This worm's turned.'

CHAPTER THIRTY-EIGHT

For the rest of the week, things at the Crown Wood Retirement Home went back to some semblance of normality, everyone running around trying to stay on top of things. Mrs Dunbar had been in touch with the care agency and they were working on getting a replacement for Draper, but that wasn't going to be a quick fix. Caring wasn't the sort of job you did for the money. It was poorly paid for the work that had to be done and there wasn't a queue of people desperate to get into the profession.

This led to the staff pulling extra hours on their shifts, and being tired contributed to little mistakes and short tempers. Bill and Charlie and a few other residents did what little they could to help: a bit of sweeping here and there; Charlie did the vacuuming; Bill also worked in the kitchen making teas and sandwiches. But the reality was that the home was drowning.

Mrs Dunbar, already up to her eyeballs, received a request from the General Medical Council for copies of all the home's current and past residents for a five-year period, and they wanted it sooner rather than later. They were conducting their own investigation into Cooper.

Susan was sitting next to Mrs Dunbar in the office. She was busy drawing up a scheduled work rota for the next month. All staff were now required to give at least fourteen days' notice if they wanted time off, and it had to be approved by Mrs Dunbar.

Bill wandered in. 'Can I get anybody a drink? Tea or coffee?'

The door buzzer went. Susan looked at the monitor: a courier. She buzzed him in.

'I'll have one in a minute, Bill,' said Susan. 'Could you do me a favour and sign for whatever this chap's delivering? Probably more meds. Shouldn't be heavy.'

'Yeah, of course.'

The courier was a big lad in heavy leathers. Over his shoulder was a large bag and, in his hand, a clipboard. Bill smiled at him, but he couldn't tell if the courier smiled back. He still wore his helmet, visor up, and Bill could only see his eyes.

'Hello, mate,' he said to Bill. 'Just the one for you today.' He pulled out a small package and put it on the table in the hall. 'If you could just give me your scribble on this bit of paper, I'll be on my way.' He handed the clipboard to Bill and then fished a pen out of his jacket pocket.

Bill peered at the paper. 'Whereabouts? My eyes are not the best.'

'Oh, sorry, mate.' The courier pointed to the name of the care home. 'Just there, please.'

'Ah, yeah. I see it,' said Bill.

The courier ripped off a copy of the document, gave it to Bill, thanked him and took off. Bill went back to the office. He set the package and duplicate of the paperwork on Susan's desk near her. She nodded a thank you, glanced over at the package and sheet, before turning back to her computer.

'You have one sugar, don't you, Mrs Dunbar?' Bill said.

'Hmm. Please, Bill. That would be nice.'

He wandered out of the office and headed for the kitchen. Ten minutes later he was back with the teas. Not a drop was spilled, thanks to the tea trolley he'd managed to forage. He'd also brought a packet of custard creams.

'There you go, ladies,' he said. 'Tea and biscuits. Good for you, they are.' He reached for Dunbar's mug. 'One sugar for you . . .'

'Thanks, Bill,' she said, not looking up from her pile of paperwork.

'And . . . one for you, Susan, my love. Biscuits too. Enjoy.'

Susan leaned across, picked up the parcel Bill had put on her desk and moved it to one side. Bill put her mug down and smiled at her. She glanced up, gave him a little smile in return and went back to work.

* * *

A couple of minutes later, Susan tore open the packet of custard creams, offered a couple to Mrs Dunbar and then took two herself. As she dunked one in her tea, she glanced at the parcel and paperwork. She looked at the two items again, for longer this time, before getting back to work.

Something niggled her.

CHAPTER THIRTY-NINE

Susan worked until eleven then told Mrs Dunbar she was going off to start getting lunch ready. Mrs Dunbar thanked her and she set off toward the kitchen. On the way, she saw Bill sitting in the lounge watching television. He was relaxing in an arm-chair, his eyes glued to the screen, his lips slightly parted. She paused at the sight of him and the stillness of the moment. He had a look of contentment on his face, as if he knew something she did not.

'Bill,' she said, 'if you're not watching anything too inter-esting, are you able to give me hand in the kitchen, please? I've got to start on getting lunch ready.'

Bill looked up at her. 'Of course. I'm only watching rubbish. Where's cook?'

'Kerry's in, but it needs at least two people to get things ready on time.'

'What do you need me to do?' he said, hauling himself up from his chair.

'I'll need a hand with the washing up and general bits and bobs. Nothing too strenuous. D'you mind?'

'Not at all. You go on ahead and I'll catch up with you in a minute. I'm a bit slower than you.' He waved her away.

'Thanks, Bill. You're a lifesaver.' She smiled and walked off toward the kitchen.

Five minutes later, Bill walked into the room. Kerry, the home's full-time cook, smiled when she saw him. 'Hello, Bill. Susan tells me you've come to give us a hand. Is that right?'

'It is indeed. What can I do to help?'

Kerry brushed at her brow with the back of her hand. 'What're you like with a knife? I need some potatoes peeled and cut into chunks, if you wouldn't mind?' She pointed to a 23 kg bag of King Edwards sitting on the floor next to the sink. Kerry was an old-school cook. She refused to use pre-peeled potatoes as a matter of principle, not trusting the process she imagined was involved.

'Not at all,' said Bill. He shuffled over to the bag.

'D'you want a stool or something, Bill?' said Susan. 'I don't want you on your feet for too long.'

'No, no. I'll be all right, my love. Don't worry about me. I'll let you know if I need to stop.'

She smiled at him. 'Alright. Thank you.'

She helped Bill open the bag of potatoes and put a big plastic bowl on the counter for the peelings. 'You sure you'll be all right?'

He waved her away. 'Tch, stop worrying about me, woman. I'm not disabled, am I?'

'No, Bill. You're right. I'm sorry. I'll get out of your way, then. Leave you to it. Kerry?'

'What, love?'

'I'm going to storage. We're a bit low on peas.'

'Alright. Can you have a look for some carrots while you're in there?'

'Of course. Won't be long. That said, it depends if I get caught by anyone needing something.'

Susan stepped out of the kitchen and ventured down the hallway that stretched before her. The floorboards creaked beneath her feet as she made her way towards the storage room. Halfway there, she paused and cast her gaze towards the lift on her right. She was about to continue on her path, but something forced her to change her mind. She reached out and pressed the button, summoning the lift to her floor. It groaned and rumbled as it made its way slowly down to her, the system designed to provide a smooth ride for the elderly residents. The doors parted with a groan and she stepped inside, pressing the button for the third floor.

A few moments later, the lift doors groaned open once again, revealing an empty hallway. She stepped out, looking left and right, taking in her surroundings. With no one in sight, she turned right and made her way down the corridor. At the end of the hall, she found the room she was searching for: Bill's. The door was locked but she had the master key, a tool all staff possessed for medical emergencies, but also for the convenience of retrieving forgotten items for the residents.

She had never done anything like this before in her life and she felt her stomach tighten into a knot. But something downstairs in the office had possessed her and was eating into her brain. She had to know if she was right or wrong. She wanted to be wrong. Her heart thumped faster and harder in her chest. Her unsteady hand fumbled the key in the lock, her heart pounding as she stepped into the darkness of Bill's room. Letting herself in, she stood in the gloom. The bed was made, sheets still tucked in from the morning, but she resisted the impulse to turn away and check the small ensuite that was tucked away in the corner. She walked across to Bill's sideboard and stopped. All of his case papers for Jack the Knife were laid out in neat order. With Draper gone, Bill saw no reason to be secretive about his obsession. Most residents knew he was an ex-police officer and those that hadn't did now.

Susan pulled the curtains open to let a bit of light in and started to look at the papers. She pulled out one or two sheets but only far enough to get a little look at them. She didn't want to take them all the way out and forget where to put it back. She thumbed through a file and found a pile of statements from potential witnesses. She went through them until she came to Bill's statements. There were a lot from him, going back a number of years. He'd been the officer in charge from the very first killing right up until the last.

Carefully, she turned the top pile of papers face down, took out one of Bill's statements and then took out her phone. She photographed the first statement, a second, third and fourth, all from different years. When she had finished, she slid back the pile of face-down papers and left the room. She could feel herself shaking.

A few minutes later, she walked back into the kitchen.

Kerry looked at her.

'What?' Susan couldn't help but feel guilty, thinking that somehow Kerry knew she'd been into Bill's room and was waiting for an answer.

'Peas? Carrots?' Kerry said.

'Oh! Bugger! Yes. Sorry! I got . . . I got caught by old Mrs Donovan. She needed some help. I did that and forgot all about the peas and carrots. What am I like?'

Bill stopped peeling and chuckled. 'Hah! That's what happens when you hang around us old'uns for too long. You'll start to forget your own name next, and from there it's a bloody short walk to losing your head completely. Back you go then, my girl, and if you're not back in ten minutes, I think we'll need to call out a search party, won't we, Kerry?'

Kerry laughed. Susan didn't.

CHAPTER FORTY

By the time the evening rolled around, Susan was exhausted. Her day wasn't over yet, though. She still had to clear up everything from the evening meal and get it all put into the dishwasher and then wait an hour until it finished, and then she had to put it all away. The night was going be a late one. She had a quick think about which of the residents might be in the lounge area but decided she couldn't keep asking them for help. She knew that they were willing enough but it didn't seem right. She'd already put a lot on Bill and Charlie. She rolled up her sleeves and got to it.

Starting in the dining room, she went around with a trolley and collected all of the dirty plates, knives, forks and spoons and loaded them onto the lower shelf of the trolley. Next came the cups: various mugs, some traditional china teacups and some plastic sippy ones for those that struggled. These all went on the top shelf — easier to pile them on top of each other without having to bend down. With the trolley full, she headed out to the kitchen and the dishwasher.

One by one, she picked up each item, rinsed it under the tap and put it into the dishwasher. She'd become proficient at packing it out in such a way that she could generally get almost everything from a full trolley into it. Anything she couldn't, she washed by hand while the machine was running.

There were a few cups and plates left that she just couldn't fit in, so she started to fill the sink. Rubber gloves on, she picked up a couple of plates and put them in the soapy water. There was just one thing left on the trolley. She picked it up, looked at it, went to put it in the water and stopped herself. She looked at it again, hesitated, then put it to one side. After a few moments, she carried on washing up the items in the sink while the washing machine droned on. On a shelf in front of her was a radio. She turned it on and listened to the presenter talking about some new situation in the Ukraine that was developing. With the stab of a button, Radio One played a song she'd never heard before and, while she tapped her foot in time to the music, something scratched at her brain. It wasn't going to go away until she did something about it.

The nagging compulsion to do something pushed her forward. Next to the freezers, Kerry the cook kept a drawer full of old bags. A quick rummage through it and Susan found a brown paper bag. It was perfect for her needs. She went back over to the sink, wondering if she was doing the right thing. This would cause a lot of problems if she was right, or she could waste a lot of people's time. She hesitated again.

What she was going to do, what she *had* to do, broke her heart.

But she did it anyway.

CHAPTER FORTY-ONE

At 9 p.m. that night, Susan finished her shift. She said good-bye to a few residents, put on her coat and checked the contents of her backpack. Taking up most of the space inside was the brown paper bag and the object she'd placed carefully inside it. She found her phone and transferred it into her coat pocket, checked that her keys were attached to the security lanyard inside the front flap of the bag, and she was ready to leave. Hauling the backpack over her shoulder she made her way out into the night.

She pulled up her hood and made her way to the bus stop a few hundred feet from the home. Her flat was on a direct route that generally took her about twenty-five minutes. Once she got off the bus, she then had a five-minute walk home. Half an hour wasn't a bad travelling time, she reasoned. It allowed her to read a few pages of her book or maybe listen to a podcast. Susan wasn't one to idly pass time when there was so much to do and learn, and she made good use of what she called 'dead time'.

Six minutes later, she was sitting on the bus with her backpack on her lap. She pulled out her phone and plugged in a set of headphones. She scrolled through until she found a podcast she'd been meaning to start for a week and hit *play*. As the intro music started, she unzipped the backpack and looked again at the brown paper bag. She felt so bad and, once more, ran it through her head whether she was doing right or wrong. The podcast host's voice began his introduction to this week's episode and she zipped the bag back up. She was decided. She was getting off the bus ten minutes early.

CHAPTER FORTY-TWO

Grace Winslet checked her watch: 11.17 a.m. She looked over the notes she'd scribbled down quickly on a pad and checked through them again before she went in to see DCI Carter. She crossed out one or two lines, rewrote them and then rewrote the whole lot out onto a new piece of paper. She wanted to make sure she was clear when she spoke to him, and had long since adopted the mantra that writing was thinking. It gave her clarity.

Ten minutes later, satisfied that things were in order, she tapped on Carter's office door, clutching her pad close to her chest.

Carter always kept his door open except for when he was in a confidential meeting, taking a confidential telephone call, giving someone a telling off or having a quick kip. He looked up from a case file he was examining. 'Come in, Gracie. Everything all right?'

'Prints have come back, guv,' she said. 'You're gonna like this.'

'Close the door and take a seat. I'm all ears.'

She shut the door, pulled out a chair and sat herself down opposite him. He stopped what he was doing and leaned back in his chair to give her his full attention. 'What you got, then?'

'Well, they belong to a Mr Leonard Clifford. But I'm going to tell you a story first. Bear with me.'

Carter nodded.

'You've heard of Jack the Knife, yes?'

'I'm familiar with it, but not in any great detail.'

'Okay. Let me remind you. Back in 1975 a young girl was brutally murdered and left in a layby on the A2. She'd been sexually assaulted and gutted. Quite literally. William Laurence Roach was a DI back then. He was the Met's golden boy at the time and was assigned to the case. Over the next twenty-odd years, the killer took the lives of at least thirty-two other women ranging from the ages of nineteen to forty-seven.

'All of these women were killed in the same or a very similar manner to the first victim. Stripped naked, multiple stab wounds, throats cut, bits removed, disembowelled. All of them had ponytails. First vic had a small tape recorder left on her body.'

'A what? A tape recorder?'

'Yep. All the subsequent vics just had the cassette, no recorder. Guess Jack wasn't made of money. So, guess what was on all of these tapes?'

'Er . . . I know this. It was an old song. Can't remember.'

'A song called "Mack the Knife". The red-top press, having a field day, nicknamed the killer "Jack the Knife". Anyway, Roach became a DCI and remained as the officer in charge throughout that twenty-odd years until the killings stopped. Just stopped. It seems DCI Roach was of the opinion that the killer was either in prison or dead. Those killings never occurred again.

'Roach worked lots of other cases at the same time. Caught them all. Couldn't catch Jack, though. There were lots of suspects. There was one bloke in particular Roach fancied for it but there was never enough evidence for an arrest. So, in 1996, Roach retires with Jack being the only one that got away. But, like many detectives who have one outstanding on the balance sheet, Roach was obsessed with catching him — *consumed* by it. Wanted to catch him before he himself died. He didn't want that unfinished one to be what he was remembered for. You wouldn't, would you?'

Carter didn't answer. He looked pensive. Winslet had seen that look many times before. She could tell he was mulling things over and writing his own story with what she was telling him.

'He still had mates in the force — went drinking with them and spent his nights out with the lads, telling them that he was still looking for Jack, still going to catch him.'

Carter sniffed and sat forward suddenly. 'Right. Hang on, I think I've got it. So, the killings stop and then Roach retires. You're telling me that DCI Roach is the killer, yes? The old boy, right?'

She frowned at him. 'Nope.'

Carter frowned. 'Go on, then.'

'DCI Roach died in 2012 aged sixty-nine.'

Carter jerked forward in his chair. 'So, who's that in the bloody care home if it's not Roach?'

'As I said, the prints tell us that he is a Mr Leonard Clifford. And Mr Leonard Clifford was the *real*, the *dead* DCI Roach's prime suspect. To the day Roach died, he was adamant it was Clifford.

'Clifford, it seems, was in fact a doctor who was struck off on suspicion of malpractice in 2011. Sexual assault on a number of his patients was one thing, another was a few suspicious deaths in a hospital. There was no evidence to charge him but that's why his prints were in the system. He was getting on a bit in years by then — sixty-eight or sixty-nine, I think — and, as far as anyone knew, he just disappeared before he could be hauled over the coals and perhaps even prosecuted. That might have opened up a whole can of worms. A few of his colleagues think he went abroad. I'll be digging into how many people died in his care later. But I have to warn you . . . it could be hundreds.'

Carter nodded. 'Go on.'

'In 2017, Leonard Clifford books himself into the Agatha Laird retirement home as DCI William Roach. We're digging into that, but I'll bet there were more deaths than usual in there too. He left there in 2018 then shows up in Crowns Woods Retirement Home, complete with a set of Jack the Knife case papers, a copy of his book and a whole new killing ground.'

'Jesus! The cheeky old git nicked the real DCI Roach's identity and just carried on killing?'

'Yep. I'm guessing that he figured the name Leonard Clifford might still pop up on the books as a cold case and that left him vulnerable to still being nicked. So, I'm betting that he took Roach's name and hid in Agatha Laird first. No one was looking for a DCI William Roach for any reason at all. He was dead. Perfect cover. Who would even think that the real DCI Roach was dead — other than people who knew him, of course? But the chances of them ever bumping into old Bill *and* knowing that he was using Roach's identity must be unbelievably small. I reckon he probably killed a good few in Agatha Laird and figured it was time to go. Turns up at Crowns Woods at the ripe old age of seventy-five. And who would suspect a likeable, fragile old man of mass murder?'

Carter sighed. 'So, once Gillian Lake's daughter, an ex-copper herself, wanted a post-mortem done, he figured his time might be limited. To take the heat off himself, he swung it onto Dr Cooper and tried to rope the Draper woman into the bargain. Then Cooper helpfully took himself out of the picture.'

'Yeah. Pretty much. That's it.'

'Do we know if anyone's dying in the home at the moment?'

'Not that I know of. Why?'

'Well, we know he won't kill anyone tonight. At 10 a.m. tomorrow, we go to Crown Woods and nick the old sod. Good work, Gracie. And we owe that Susan Johnson a bloody good drink.'

CHAPTER FORTY-THREE

Bill woke up at 2 a.m. After ten minutes of lying in the dark, he knew he wasn't going to back to sleep anytime soon. After a short struggle, he pulled himself upright and sat there looking at the rain running down his windowpane. Though he fought to keep his eyes open, he knew that if he laid back down he wouldn't sleep. It was his pattern. Had been for many years. He pulled back his duvet cover and shivered in the chill of the room.

Crown Woods turned the heating down during the night to conserve both energy and money. It made sense. Most of the residents were in bed by 10 p.m., tucked up under their duvets. For residents like Bill, who woke up or couldn't even get to sleep until the very small hours, it could be a chilly time.

He picked up the dressing gown he kept at the foot of his bed and pulled it on before standing himself upright. He wobbled a bit as he tried to gain his balance. Once he had it, he decided that he would go downstairs into the kitchen, make himself a cup of tea and watch a bit of mindless early hours TV.

The home was deathly quiet. As he neared the lift, he could hear the drone of a TV set from behind Room 42. He smiled to himself. Mrs Davis had fallen asleep in front of the box again. It was a good thing most of the residents were hard of hearing.

He got out of the lift on the ground floor and made his way into the kitchen, ready for his tea. It surprised him to see another resident standing at the kitchen counter waiting for the kettle to boil. Albert Walsh was about the same age as Bill and a relative newcomer to Crown Woods. He and Bill got on, but it was more of a "how do you do?" kind of a relationship, where they would pass the time of day with each other for ten minutes or so but leave it at that.

'Morning, Bill,' said Albert. 'Couldn't sleep?'

Bill gave a slight wave. 'Morning. Nope. Lay about seeing if I could get back but it was a waste of time. Thought I'd have a cuppa. See if that helped.'

'I know what you mean. I'll make you a cuppa if you like?'

'Yeah?'

'Yeah, course. I'm making one for myself so one more's not a problem, is it? Where are you going to sit? Here or in the lounge?'

Bill stopped and nodded. Wherever he sat it was going to be a bit fresh, but at least the lounge always had a few blankets he could put around himself to keep the chill out. 'Lounge. Might watch the telly, see what's going on.'

'Alright, mate. Won't be long.'

'Thanks, Albert. Very kind of you.'

Bill shuffled off to the lounge and sat himself in a big armchair directly in line with the TV. He forgot the remote and, after a few choice mutterings, hauled himself up and made his way over to the shelf that housed the device. He'd barely sat back down when Albert came in with two mugs of steaming-hot tea on a tray. He set his down on the table and handed Bill's to him.

'Ta.' Bill took it and looked at it. 'Sorry, Albert. Don't mean to be a fuss pot, but I prefer to use my own mug. I should have said.'

189

Albert struggled to hide the fact that he couldn't understand Bill's reasoning. *A mug's a mug, so just drink it, you silly old sod.*

Bill caught it. 'I know. It sounds silly, but it's a habit. I've had that mug for years and it's one of those daft things that bothers me. I'm sorry.'

'That's okay,' said Albert. 'Give us it here and I'll pour it into your mug.'

'Are you sure? I don't mean to be a nuisance.'

'Don't be daft, Bill. C'mon, give it here.'

Bill handed over the mug and Albert walked back to the kitchen. Bill half heard what was probably chuntering when Albert thought he was out of earshot. Bill pressed the remote and watched the telly spark into life. He scooched back into the chair and made himself comfortable while he waited for his tea to reappear.

Albert came back in carrying the same mug as before. 'Sorry, Bill. Can't find yours anywhere. I've had the cupboards out and the little dishwasher. Can't find it. Sorry.'

Bill was more than a little miffed. 'Really? That's annoying. Wonder where it's gone, then?'

Albert shrugged. He clearly thought he'd done his bit. He got on with Bill, but probably not enough to go raking around for his 'special mug' again. He was done. 'Dunno. Probably someone's picked it up by accident and taken it off to their room. We've all done it. I wouldn't worry about it.' He sat himself down in the chair next to Bill and looked at the TV to see what was on. A cooking show at nearly three in the morning. Of course there was.

'Yeah, but you know what mine's like. It's made of tin with a Pepsi logo on it. It's pretty hard to mistake.'

Albert kept his eyes on the TV. 'Sorry, Bill. Don't know what to tell you. It wasn't there and I did look properly.'

'Yeah, yeah. I know. I appreciate it. Thank you. I wonder where it's gone, then? That'll bug me now until it shows up. Bugger it!'

Bill took a sip from the ceramic mug. He was not a happy man.

CHAPTER FORTY-FOUR

Bill and Charlie were sitting at the kitchen table drinking tea when Susan started her shift at eight thirty in the morning the next day. Both gave her a little wave. She spotted Bill drinking from his own mug and breathed a sigh of relief. Winslet had made good on her promise to get it back.

'Morning, Susan,' Bill said. 'How are you today?'

'Morning, love,' said Charlie.

Susan gave them both a smile. 'Morning, boys. How are we doing?' She checked the weight of the kettle and filled it up again. 'I take it you both want tea?'

They did.

She spotted the empty plates in front of them. 'You've had breakfast already, then?'

'Yep,' said Charlie. 'Bloody lovely it was. Fry-up.'

She chuckled. 'Same with you, Bill?'

Bill nodded but said nothing. Susan felt her stomach tighten.

'What're you both up to today? Anything good planned? Either of you going out anywhere?'

Both shook their heads.

'I can't be bothered,' said Charlie. 'Bloody weather's awful, isn't it? Soddin' rain gets on me nerves.'

'I take your point,' she said. 'Bill?'

He shook his head again. 'No, I'm staying in. Got something planned.'

Charlie frowned at the pair of them.

Susan brought the teas over and sat herself down opposite Bill. She handed out the teas and sat back in her chair, arms crossed against her chest. They sat in silence for a full minute until Charlie couldn't stand it anymore.

'This is nice, isn't it? Three old pals havin' a good old chat. Lovely.' He blew into his cup and took a sip of his tea. 'You two carry on. Don't let me interrupt you.' He sat back in his chair and looked at the two of them.

Neither said anything. The atmosphere was strained between Bill and Susan, and Charlie was getting irritated by it.

'Right, what is it? What's up with you two? You normally get on like a house on fire. What's happened?'

Bill didn't look at him. He shook his head as an answer.

Susan felt awkward at being called out. 'Nothing,' she said.

'Nothing, is it? Okay, then. It's just that I can literally feel the atmosphere between the pair of you. I know something's gone on between you, so what is it?'

'Nothing,' said Susan. She was firmer this time. 'I'm not in the mood to talk, that's all.'

'What?' said Charlie. 'Why? You're always talking.'

'Lady time, all right? Now leave it, Charlie.'

Charlie wrinkled his nose. 'No, it's not that, and *eew*! No need for that, was there? I'm a man of a certain age and where I come from, women don't say that sort of thing.' He stood up. 'So, on that little note, I'm gonna let you sort it out between yourselves. See you both later. Ta-ta.' He pushed his chair back under the table and left them both to it.

'You all right, then?' said Bill, without really looking at her.

'Yeah. As I said, I don't feel too well today. Dodgy belly.'

'Lady time, you said. That can be nasty.'

'Hmm. How's you, then?'

192

'Mustn't grumble.'

'Hmm.' She sipped at her tea.

'I came down for a drink in the night. Couldn't find my cup. Bloody annoyed me, that did.'

Susan felt her stomach tighten even more and her head spun for a second. 'You've got it now, though. Where was it?'

'No idea. I swear it wasn't there when we looked for it.'

'We?'

'Me and Albert Walsh. He made the tea but couldn't find my mug anywhere. I had to use another one. Didn't taste the same.'

'Really? It's just tea, Bill.'

He turned and looked at her. 'Didn't taste the same.'

She nodded. 'Well, you've got it now, so all is right with the world, eh?'

'Is it? It isn't for me. I don't like people taking my things. Never have.'

Susan stiffened. 'I'm sure it was just a mistake, Bill. Whoever took it must have realised and put it back this morning. They're probably mortified. Everyone knows you only like your own mug. Just a mistake. I'm sure someone will apologise to you later.'

Bill nodded. 'You think so?'

'I'm sure they will. You'll see.'

'I hope so, Susan. I really do. I get so angry when people do stuff and don't own up to it.'

Susan caught his expression. He wasn't kidding.

CHAPTER FORTY-FIVE

It was 9.30 a.m. when Jenny Teach, senior care worker at Crown Woods, heard the main entrance buzzer go. 'Can I help you?' Jenny said into the intercom.

'It's Jackie Draper. Lemme in.'

'Do you have an appointment?' said Jenny.

'Don't be bloody funny. Just lemme in. Now!'

'Certainly. Report to the office.' Jenny pressed a buzzer and let Draper into the building. She made her way directly to Dunbar's office and banged on the door. Jenny opened it and the two women glared at each other.

Jenny Teach had had her fair share of run-ins with Draper and she was over the moon when she heard the woman had been arrested and sacked. She was about the same age as Draper and came from a similar background. Abusive family, abusive husband — she'd got rid of him, though. A single mum of two boys herself, she was not in the slightest bit intimidated by Draper. In fact, she once had her by the throat in the locker room and threatened to 'scar' her if she ever bad-mouthed her again. Draper knew she was serious from that point on and studiously avoided her. Now they were face to face again.

'I'm going to get my things,' Draper said.

'No, you're not,' said Jenny. 'You're waiting here until Mrs Dunbar shows up with your things. They've been dumped into a bag for when you rolled up.'

Draper scowled. 'What? That old bitch better not have damaged my stuff.'

Jenny shrugged. 'Nah, not her way. She's too nice. Me, though, I broke a few things. Just for fun.'

Draper glared at her, but Jenny was deliberately pushing her buttons, knowing that Draper was out on bail and would likely go straight inside if she tried anything — quite apart from the fact that Jenny would likely beat her senseless. She did, however, try to intimidate Jenny by standing in her personal space and staring at her.

Calm and collected, Jenny smiled at her. 'Get out of my face, you skank, before I smack you into a coma.'

Draper backed away, saving face in part by the arrival of Mrs Dunbar. She wasn't hanging around and walked straight past the two women, seemingly oblivious to the animosity between them.

'Mrs Draper,' said Mrs Dunbar, 'in my office. You too, Jenny. I want you to witness and record what's being returned to her, if you wouldn't mind.'

Jenny nodded. 'Pleasure.'

Draper sneered at Jenny and turned to Mrs Dunbar. She saw she was holding a black bin liner and that little fact plainly irked her. She stepped into the office just as Dunbar dropped the bag onto her desk. Jenny walked in behind and closed the door.

'Careful with my stuff, Dunbar,' said Draper. 'Don't you break anything.'

Mrs Dunbar ignored her and opened the bag. 'Can you make a note of these items, please, Jen?' She handed her a clipboard with a sheet of white A4 paper on it. She took out the first item. 'One pink-coloured bag containing various used items of makeup.'

Jenny wrote it down, and for the next six minutes faithfully recorded everything Mrs Dunbar pulled out of the plastic sack.

'That's everything, then,' said Mrs Dunbar. 'Your money will be made up to the day you were dismissed and paid into your account on the normal pay date.'

Draper nodded. 'Where's my mug and plate?'

Mrs Dunbar shrugged. 'Mug? Plate? I have no idea.'

'Did you look for them?' said Draper.

'Didn't think about it. Thanks to you, I've had a serious increase in my workload.'

'Boo-bloody-hoo,' said Draper. 'I left them in the cupboard in the kitchen. They better still be there, or else I'll sue you.'

Jenny chuckled. 'For what? One pound, seventy-five pence? That'll be a laugh in court.'

Mrs Dunbar sighed. 'Really? A mug and a plate?'

'Belongs to me. My property. I'm not leaving it here for any of these wrinkly old bags of filth to use. I'm gonna go get them.' She turned abruptly to find her way deliberately blocked by Jenny.

'You're not wandering around in here,' said Jenny. 'I'll go and get them.' She looked over Draper's shoulder to Mrs Dunbar. 'That all right with you?'

'We'll all go,' said Mrs Dunbar. 'Keep an eye on her.' In truth, Mrs Dunbar probably didn't fancy being left alone with Draper. Jenny shrugged, stepped aside to let Draper past and then followed her outside. Mrs Dunbar closed the office door and led the way to the kitchen.

CHAPTER FORTY-SIX

Bill looked at Susan, his eyes heavy with emotion. He reached for his mug, pausing as he reflected on his feelings for her. Despite the large age gap, he couldn't help the affection he felt. It confused him, but it also brought him a sense of joy he'd never had before.

He drained his mug and let out a sigh. 'That was lovely. Probably my last cuppa, that.'

Susan's body stiffened in response.

'So. You caught me, eh?'

She sat bolt upright.

'I know what you did, Susan. With my mug. You took it to Grace Winslet, yes?'

She nodded as a tear escaped her eye.

'Look, don't worry. It's okay. Really. You did what you had to do.'

'I . . . I didn't . . . I . . . I was scared, Bill. Confused. I'm so sorry.'

'Scared?' Bill was both surprised and hurt at the suggestion, but he knew she had a point. His reputation went before him.

'You didn't have to be scared of me, Susan. I would never in a million months of Sundays have hurt you.' He shook his head. 'I wouldn't have. Not you.'

Susan began to hyperventilate as anxiety overtook her. Bill had seen that look so many times before on the faces of his victims. It gave him a little thrill for a second.

'Susan. Susan, please. Don't be scared. I'm not going to hurt you, I promise.'

Susan nodded quickly, tears now rolling down her cheeks. Bill felt a lump in his throat. Not something he'd ever felt before. He shook his head as if that might loosen it.

'It's okay. You did the right thing. I wish you hadn't, but there we are. Funny, though . . . I thought I might actually make it to my grave without getting caught. Never mind.'

Susan sobbed. A big heaving sob from her chest. 'Bill . . .'

'When are they coming for me?'

She sobbed again. 'I . . . I don't know. Soon?' She shrugged.

'Okay. Not to worry. You, young lady . . . you should be very proud of yourself.'

Susan took a big sniff. Bill handed her his handkerchief. Clean. Neatly pressed. She took it from him and dabbed at her nose before blowing it. 'Why?'

He chuckled. 'Because you, you managed to do what the combined might of the Metropolitan Police failed to do for, what? Best part of fifty years. You caught me. Jack the Knife. A girl in her twenties. No police experience at all. Outstanding work. Right, c'mon, tell me . . . What gave me away?'

She sniffed again and wiped her eyes with the back of her hand. 'It was your signature. The parcel you signed for, remember? I'd been reading your book the night before and I saw the photos in there. One had DCI Roach's signature on the bottom of a report. I dunno. An alarm bell went off in my head. I compared the two signatures and then again with the one you wrote in the cover. And they were so different. It got me thinking.' She lowered her head. 'I'm . . . so sorry, Bill.'

'Go on,' he said.

'I just couldn't shake it. Then I got to thinking about what you said about Dr Cooper always visiting just before a patient died. But you were there when every patient died, weren't you? We all thought you were being kind, but you weren't, were you? You were killing them.'

Bill smiled. 'Hmm.'

'Why, Bill? Why do that?'

He sighed deeply before answering. 'I honestly don't know, Susan. I don't. I used to be a doctor—'

'What?' said Susan. 'A . . . doctor?'

'Yeah. I qualified as a junior when I was just twenty-three. Very young. I killed the first one when I was . . . twenty-four, I think it was. Don't know why. I just did. It gave me a thrill.'

Susan winced. 'Oh, Bill . . .'

'I know. Anyway, I was horrified at first but, as I said, thrilled at what I'd done. So, I did it again. And again. I did it through all of my career.' He watched a tear roll down Susan's cheek. 'I'm sorry. I am.'

'How many people did you kill, Bill?'

'A lot. Too many to count. Too many to remember.'

'Oh, God . . . Bill . . . How did you not get caught?'

He raised his head. 'We were gods. Doctors back in the day were quite literally gods. Nobody questioned us, not thoroughly anyway. What we said went. If anybody questioned us, there were a thousand excuses why someone died, and the hierarchy didn't look into things too deeply back then. You know yourself . . . Harold Shipman. Look how many he killed. Hundreds. The thing is, he wasn't the only one doing it, and I certainly wasn't.'

'Oh, my dear God,' said Susan. It seemed as if the air went out of her body and her frame collapsed.

'So,' said Bill, 'you know when they say, "lessons will be learned"? Well, the next time you hear that, know that they don't get learned. I carried on for a number of years after Shipman. It was more difficult, I grant you, but it never stopped me. So, while I was a young doctor and was getting this thrill, it became an addiction for me. But, like any addiction, it grew in its hunger. I wasn't content with just killing people as I had been doing. I needed a bigger thrill, a bigger fix. So, I took a knife—'

'Stop, Bill! I can't take any more. Please, stop.' She got up from her seat.

Leonard Clifford looked at her. 'Sit . . . back . . . down, Susan. You caught me, now you get to hear my story.'

His tone must have startled her. She did as she was told, trembling slightly.

Bill closed his eyes, remembering fondly. 'It carried on from there. I couldn't help myself. After the first knife killing, I went back to doing patients, but it was like . . . it was like eating hamburgers after having filet mignon. Nowhere near the same thing. Nowhere near it. And I just kept getting away with it. DCI Roach, though, he was good. He nearly had me a few times.'

He shook his head. 'My real name is Leonard Clifford. Roach was the officer tasked to hunt me down. He dragged me in for questioning a few times, but had to let me go. You see, I was good at what I did, Susan. I never left anything that could tie me to the case. Forensics was a different game back then, but I kept myself up to date with advances in crime detection methods and developments in the field of forensics. Roach was smart. I was smarter.

'He died a while back without ever catching me. So, when I decided I was getting too old to kill people with a knife, I adapted. That's what animals do if they want to survive. I "retired", went into an old people's home and used a new method.'

Susan closed her eyes and shook her head. 'What was it?'

'Air. We need it to live, but it can also kill. So, when I came here, I told Mrs Dunbar that I had a condition that required me to inject myself on a daily basis . . . diabetes. I also told her that I had Addison's disease. Both were a lie. I don't have either — never have. Why did I say that? Well, people with type 2 diabetes may require an injection every day. Those with Addison's only need an injection if they have what's known as an "adrenal crisis". But both gave me a good reason to be in possession of a hypodermic needle. I made a point of carrying my little injection kit around with me every day, telling people all about me having these medical problems and that I may have to give myself an urgent injection or I could die.

'I made a point of putting the kit bag on the table when I had breakfast, lunch, dinner, whenever. It drew a few questions at first and then everybody just stopped seeing it. It became invisible. Once they did that, I knew I could begin.'

'Christ . . .' said Susan. 'I never gave it a thought.'

'Why would you? It wasn't your responsibility to check that I really had these diseases, was it? No. It was Mrs Dunbar's. She's a lovely woman, she really is. And that's her weakness. She's naïve and takes everything she's told at face value.

'I was careful about the people I killed in here, though. I took only those who were very ill. Suffering. Those whose remaining life would only have been even more miserable than it already was. I did them a favour, really.'

'By killing them? You have no right to make that judgement. You have no right to decide who lives and who dies.'

'And yet, I do. I've done it since I was a lad. Who stopped me? Not God. Not the police. I made the decision to end their lives. I had that right in the absence of God. So, despite what I did to the others — and there's no excuse for any of that — when I went to sit with the people who I went on to kill, I believed that it was a good thing. You see, there are no assisted suicide programmes in this country yet and some people suffer, *really* suffer in dire agony. Sometimes for years. And they shouldn't. They should be allowed to choose when they go. I was trying to do something good, both by being with them at the end and taking away their miserable existence. I know you won't believe that, but it's true.'

Susan could only shake her heard at his little speech. 'I don't believe you, Bill. *They* should choose. Not you. You murdered these people just like you did to all the others. Different method, same result. You're a serial killer, Bill. That's all. There's no compassion. You lied. You lied to everyone. To me. You just found another outlet because you're too old and weak to kill any other way.'

Bill looked over at her, genuinely sad that he'd destroyed the only good relationship with a woman, with a human, he'd ever had. He looked up at the sound of people coming along the hall. Draper, Mrs Dunbar and Jenny Teach were coming toward the kitchen.

'Oh, Susan,' he said. 'I'm nowhere near as weak as you think.'

Susan looked puzzled. Even more so when Bill stood upright. No struggle, no groans, no reaching for his stick. Straight up. Effortless.

'I have something to do, Susan. You might want to go now and call Carter and Winslet.'

'What? Bill? How . . . I thought you were . . .'

Bill smiled.

Susan snapped her head around sharply. 'Oh, Christ!' she had spotted an angry-faced Jackie Draper.

'Call them, Susan. It's okay.' He gave an almost serene smile.

'Oi, copper!' Draper shouted. She clearly hadn't registered that Bill was standing tall, unaided. Neither had the other two.

'Don't you start, Draper.' Jenny's voice was sharp. Hard.

'This is you, innit? You did this to me. You fitted me up, you filthy scumbag!'

Jenny grabbed her arm as a rage overtook Draper. Draper spun and pushed her in the chest, knocking her backward and over, then turned back to Bill and went for him.

As she advanced on him, Bill put both hands casually in his pocket and watched her. When Draper was within arm's length and coming fast, he pulled out a knife, ducked under Draper's arm, came up and grabbed her by the throat. In one quick move, he spun her around and dropped her onto the table, on her back.

Susan screamed and leaped backward out of her chair as Draper's legs flailed in her direction. Jenny was struggling to get up, looking shocked at what she was witnessing, and Mrs Dunbar simply stood open-mouthed.

Flat on her back, Draper must have felt the cold pressure of the knife against her throat as Bill's bony fingers dug deep into her skin. He was conscious of filling up with a familiar and empowering rage. His lips pulled back in a sneer and a drop of spittle fell from his mouth onto her face. Her bladder emptied involuntarily as his hot breath fell onto her cheeks, and he growled in her face, 'Are you ready, bitch?'

Draper couldn't breathe. Her eyes were wide, fixated on Bill's, so close to her own.

'I've killed many women, bitch, but you . . . You I will truly enjoy. I'm gonna gut you and pull your filthy, rancid innards out, you nasty, no-good piece of filth!'

'Bill, don't!' Susan screamed at him. 'Don't! Please. Please don't.'

Bill ignored her for a full ten seconds. A lifetime. 'Call them, Susan. Do as I tell you. Do it now!'

Susan hesitated, unsure at first of what he meant. Then she ran to the office.

Jenny, now on her feet, and Mrs Dunbar stood paralysed with fear.

'Mrs Dunbar!' Bill shouted. Jenny! Get out of here! Now!' He never turned to them, kept his face pressed against Draper's.

'Bill . . .' said Jenny. 'Please don't do this . . .'

Bill sucked in a deep breath. His shoulders lifted. 'Now!' he shouted. 'Do it now!'

They ran out of the kitchen.

Bill dragged Draper up from the table, knife still against her throat. 'Surprised, bitch?' He grinned at her 'I wouldn't blame you. Ah, old Bill. Thin as a rake, doddery on his feet, frightened to say anything back. Old Bill, who let you bully him because he couldn't fight back. Too weak. Too frail.' He dragged her over to the kitchen units and put his back against the broom cupboard. He pulled Draper in front of him, pulled her tight against him. 'Seems you slipped up, eh? Seems you misjudged me? Seems you had no clue that I'm Jack the Knife. Until now. You dozy bitch, I pretended to be

203

the sick, frail man you wanted to see, to live up to the stereotype of an aged one-foot-in-the-grave pensioner. You know what that did, bitch? Made me invisible, that's what that did. And it brought out your true nature for all to see. And you know what? You're right. I did fit you up. So damned easy too. No one suspects me, do they? No. Not old Bill. He can come and go. Take no notice of him. And they didn't. And I watched. And I knew where the keys to the drug cabinet were kept. And picking the lock on your locker was a doddle. Two bottles of morphine. Thank you very much. Easy.'

He chuckled in her ear. 'Oh, Draper, my little bitch. Today has been momentous. Absolutely momentous. And it's going to be even more so. Do you know why?'

She shivered her head in her response, clearly too scared to shake it properly.

'No, of course you don't. Too stupid to appreciate what's going on. Let me tell you, then. Today is the day Susan caught the infamous serial killer Jack the Knife. Susan! Who would have thought it? Did you? Would you have thought it? No. Of course you wouldn't. And . . . this is the good bit for you. You get to go down in history. You get to be Jack's last ever victim. How good is that?'

Bill felt the weight of Draper's body crumble in front of him as her legs gave out. She moaned deeply, like a trapped animal who knows it's time has finally come.

Bill opened up a small cut on her neck. 'What a bloody glorious day!'

CHAPTER FORTY-SEVEN

DS Grace Winslet was shrugging on her coat when her mobile phone, lying on her desk, rang. She tutted and looked at the caller ID: Susan Johnson.

'Hello—' She was cut off by the terrified voice of Susan, shouting hysterically down the phone at her.

'Susan? Susan, what is it? What's wrong?'

She started toward Carter's office, trying to get a word in against Susan's panicked voice.

'Susan! Stop! Slow down, I don't understand . . .'

Carter looked up on hearing Winslet's voice. He rose, agitated, his face showing concern. He looked at her curiously. In the doorway, Grace pointed to the phone against her ear and mouthed, *Susan Johnson*. Carter nodded.

'Okay. Okay. Slow down. He's what? What's happening?' Her eyes widened. 'Stay away from him, Susan. You hear me? Stay away!'

Carter rose from his desk and slipped his jacket on. In the main office, three of his team stared at Grace.

'We're on our way, Susan. We're coming!' She stabbed at the phone and ended the call. Before Carter could ask, she spat it out. 'It's Bill. He's got a knife against Draper's throat. He's going to kill her!'

Carter rounded his desk and followed Winslet. 'At the home?'

'Yes,' she said, running now. The three other detectives all rose and ran with her.

Carter broke into a run. 'Colin! Call the shots out. I want SCO19 there. Now!'

Colin Styles picked up the phone. He knew the number by heart.

'And ring downstairs. Find out if any plods are nearby. They're not to approach. Contain only.'

Running down the stairs two at a time, he muttered to himself, 'This isn't gonna end well.'

CHAPTER FORTY-EIGHT

DCI Carter forced his car through the traffic. Unmarked but equipped with blue lights and siren, he bullied other drivers out of the way until he broke free from the herd and pushed the pedal to the floor. Next to him, Grace was listening intently to the radios: one connected to local units, one connected to the control room at New Scotland Yard. It had been some time since she'd taken on the role of a vehicle radio operator and had forgotten just how intense it could be.

Behind them, in a separate car, the rest of the squad were doing exactly the same, dodging and weaving while staying glued to the back of Carter's car, using him as the push car. In the distance, she could hear other sirens all heading to Crown Woods.

'*MP, MP, Hotel One two minutes away,*' came a male voice on the radio. Grace didn't recognise the voice. She knew Hotel One was the fast response car. It had a two-man crew.

'*Thank you,*' said a female controller at Scotland Yard; its call sign was MP. '*Approach with caution, Hotel One. Suspect is armed and dangerous. SCO19 are on way. ETA eight minutes. DCI Carter, your ETA, please?*' The voice of MP was calm, fully in control. Nothing phased her.

'Sergeant Winslet speaks, MP,' said Grace. 'Five minutes.'

'*Thank you, sergeant,*' said MP. '*First unit on scene, update please.*' The radio went silent just as the scream of Carter's siren cut through Winslet's ears. Adrenaline flooded her body as the excitement rose within her. This was what the job was about. The excitement of rushing toward a situation whose outcome was unknown. This excitement is what drove police officers on. It was why there were highly trained area car drivers at each station: to be there quicker than anyone else, to be first on scene. The buzz was their drug of choice.

Winslet's radio crackled. '*Hotel One. Thirty seconds.*'

'*Thank you, Hotel One.*'

'Carter and Winslet. Two minutes.' She hooked the radio back into its cradle and prepared herself for a rapid exit from the car.

As they pulled up, she saw that Hotel One's front doors were wide open, the crew so eager to attend the scene that closing the doors would have used up a whole second they may not have to save someone's life.

She and Carter ran into the foyer and saw a visibly shaken Susan Johnson in Dunbar's office.

'Where is he?' Grace shouted.

'Kitchen!' Susan shouted back.

They kept running until they saw the crew of Hotel One standing by the doors. Winslet could see Draper in the distance. Her face was etched with terror. Behind her, pulled in tight, was Bill, his knife against her throat.

* * *

Grace and Carter took up pole position in the doorway, having relegated the crew of Hotel One to second place behind them. Grace looked at Bill and didn't like what she saw looking back at her. His face was very different. Gone were the tired features of a wizened old man waiting to die. In their place was a renewed vigour, a vibrancy, a look of purpose. She was dumbfounded that he was standing so straight now

— tall, his feet planted firmly and his wiry arms looking full of strength.

He was waiting for her as she stepped into the room.

'Grace! Wait!' said Carter.

She held up her hand as she began to walk toward Bill. 'It's okay,' she said.

Carter took a step into the room behind her but kept his distance. He no doubt thought that his presence might intimidate Bill, cause him to panic and do something drastic.

* * *

Carter didn't know his enemy. Bill wasn't one to panic. Never had been. Nor was he intimidated by Carter being there. What he wasn't happy about was the fact that the two of them might take up position either side of him, think about it, and maybe try to rush him.

He knew that his day was done, but he didn't want them to do anything foolish. Not yet. Draper was done for. That was decided, and she would lose her life today, one way or the other. He would too. It didn't bother him, dying. He had seen so much death, had been responsible for so many deaths that it meant nothing to him. His philosophy of life left no room for any possibility of a better place, a God, or anyone or anything that might offer him some form of redemption when he died. It didn't exist for him, so what was there to be scared of if there was no one to answer to?

'Hello, Bill,' said Winslet. 'What's going on with you, then? This all looks a bit messy.'

'Hello, Gracie. You made it here, then?' He pulled Draper tighter into him.

'Oh, yeah. Soon as we could. Traffic was ropey. You know how it is.'

Bill nodded. 'I do. You people don't hang around when there's a chance of catching Britain's biggest ever serial killer, do you? Who's going to grab the medal, eh? You? Or what about you, Mr Carter? Which one is it?'

Winslet shrugged. 'It's not about medal's, Bill. Never is. It's about catching you bad boys. That's the reward.'

Bill chuckled. 'Hmm. Maybe, Gracie. Maybe. Where's Susan?'

Winslet glanced over her shoulder. 'Last I saw of her, she was in Dunbar's office. She didn't look good, Bill. Looked frightened out of her life.'

'Ah . . . Poor Susan. Didn't mean to frighten her. I really didn't, but . . . you know how it is.'

Winslet nodded at him. 'Yeah, I do. Shame, though. I mean, she thinks the world of you, Bill. She talks so fondly of you, y'know? I think she loves you a little bit, if I'm honest. She's lovely that one, and you've gone and frightened seven sacks of crap out of her. Probably damaged her for life, you have.'

Bill's expression softened. 'I know. I'm so sorry. I didn't want it to come to this.'

Winslet shifted her eyes toward Draper, probably looking to see if she had any fight left in the tank, whether she would be able to respond if Winslet or Carter gave her a command of some sort. But she hadn't and she couldn't. She was beyond help. She'd given up.

Carter inched closer.

'Harry!' Bill said. 'Don't do it. Do not! If you're planning to launch some sort of misguided heroic attempt to save her, don't. I will drive this knife underneath her jaw, up and into her brain before you can shout "no"!'

Draper whimpered. Bill kissed her on the top of the head. 'There, there, bitch. Keep it together. Remember what I told you. History.'

'What's that mean, Bill?' said Winslet.

He smiled at her. 'I was telling her that she'll be famous. She'll be Jack the Knife's last victim.'

Winslet tensed up. It had dawned on her that he was going to do it. No doubt about it. 'No, you don't, Bill. I can't let you do that.' She was putting on a brave face, he had to give her that.

He smirked at her. 'What? You can't *let* me? How are you going to stop me, Gracie?' He whipped the knife away from Draper's throat and pushed it against her back. She arched forward as the point pressed into her. 'You're not in a position to stop anything, my love.'

He pushed it in, slowly. Jackie shrieked in pain as the blade dug in. Blood trickled down the back of her blouse. Carter jerked forward. Bill spun her around toward him, his eyes fixed on Carter, willing him to try.

'Nothing . . . you . . . can . . . do.'

Once Winslet saw the blood drip onto the floor, she raised her hands. 'Bill! Don't! Please!'

He stopped, and pivoted them both to face Winslet.

'Bill. Why'd you pretend to be a copper? Why Roach?'

He sucked in a deep breath before he spoke. 'Honestly?'

'Yeah. Honestly.'

'I admired him. I truly did. We came face to face on a few occasions. Interviews and statements, that sort of thing. He was sharp, clever and bloody tenacious. My God, that man came for me, and I respected that, y'know? Billy was a good man. A decent man. He knew it was me. Knew it from the off. Just couldn't prove it. But, in all the times we bumped heads, he never tried to physically intimidate me. Never laid a finger on me. Never treated me badly. Just worked on me psychologically. Lied to me a few times, but that was to be expected if he wasn't willing to beat a confession out of me, I suppose.

'We kept tabs on each other over the years, and when I saw in the papers he'd died, I thought there was no better way to honour such a noble man than by taking his identity. Then I thought it would be a good idea if everyone thought that I was still hunting Jack. Takes the whole thing to a different level, if that makes sense?'

Winslet frowned. 'No. No, it doesn't. That makes no sense at all. How can you hunt yourself?'

Bill shook his head. 'No, no, no, no. I wasn't hunting myself, Gracie. I was honouring him and his hunt for me.

I let people know that DCI Bill Roach was still looking for Jack the Knife and would never give up. Y'see?'

Winslet nodded. 'Okay. But it's mental, Bill. I mean . . . come on.'

Bill shrugged.

'Where did you get all of his papers from? Your case file?'

He nodded. 'It was the day of the funeral. I didn't think I'd be welcome there, so I took the opportunity to break in to his house while everybody was saying goodbye to him. I ransacked the place and found the files. To be honest, it wasn't hard. They were on his desk along with one of those murder maps you guys use. The ones with bits of strings and suspects pinned up for reference.

'His widow couldn't call the police because she knew Billy shouldn't have had them. Not much she could do.'

'She must have known it was you who broke in.'

'Hmm. I expect she did.'

'You must have scared her witless, Bill.'

'Yeah, I know. But she was safe. I wouldn't hurt her. Not his wife. I had to respect that.'

'What's the story with the tapes? Why that song?'

Bill smiled. 'Well, believe it or not, I just loved it. That's all. Oh, and I used to play it while I was killing people. It cheered me up. Killing is a pretty grim business, y'know? You need something to keep your spirits up.'

Winslet shook her head. 'Jesus Christ, Bill!'

'It's the truth. Sorry it's nothing more interesting.'

'Tell me about the people you killed at the home. How did you do it?'

Bill twisted the knife that was in Draper's back. She screamed in pain as he smiled.

'Bill, don't!' shouted Winslet. 'Please, please, don't do that. Just stop. All right? Stop!'

Bill sniffed and did as she asked. 'My hypodermic. Air.'

'I figured something like it. But how the hell do you do that?'

'It's not difficult injecting air into a vein to cause death. An air embolus, it's called. Look, in order to kill a person, all you need is about 100 to 200 cc, that's roughly the equivalent of a cup of air injected into a vein. It's what I call the Goldilocks method of killing — you need just the right amount. Too little air and the victim might feel a bit rough for a while, but they won't die. Too much air and they die way too quickly. So, it's all about finding that sweet spot. Fun fact for you, Gracie: most people think this method involves injecting air into the arteries, but that's not the case. Arteries pump blood away from the heart, while veins carry it towards the heart, and when it gets there . . . Boom! Out go the lights. Only a full post-mortem would reveal such a large mass of air in the right ventricle, and they'd know straight away that they'd been injected.'

'Hence why you didn't want Gillian Lake to have a PM.'

'Yep.'

Winslet held a hand up. 'Okay, I've got it. So, correct me if I'm wrong, you knew the likelihood of them having a PM was very low. Even less chance of it if they'd been seen by a doctor and examined shortly before they died. Hence why you always killed them within, what? Thirty-six hours of Cooper's examination?'

Bill grinned.

'So, yeah,' said Winslet, 'on the surface, they all died of age-related diseases. Cooper knew they were ill, death may have been a bit surprising but not really unexpected, so no need for a PM. You slippery old sod. So, did you make them ill so Cooper would come out?'

'Sometimes. If the craving was too bad. But mostly, I knew when he was coming. It was regular. I would make them ill a few days beforehand and send them to their beds. They would get weak. *Very* weak. Maybe what I used exacerbated their underlying health problems, I'm not sure about that. Bonus if it did.'

'What did you use to make them ill?'

Bill smiled again, pleased with himself. 'Foxglove. A natural poison. Use enough of it and it can kill. Use the right amount . . . sickness. Takes a bit of time to get it into the system but, what else is there to do but drink tea all day?'

Carter looked alarmed. 'Ah, Jesus wept, Bill. Have you poisoned anyone else in here?'

Bill smiled. 'Maybe. I've made you tea, remember?'

Winslet looked thoughtful. She'd had a few cups on her visits. 'You're screwing with me, old man.'

Bill chuckled loudly. 'Chance would be a fine thing, Gracie.'

Carter lurched forward again. 'You wicked old sod!'

'Ah-ah, Harry! Down boy!' He pulled Draper around to face him. Carter stopped.

'That's why you kept your own mug all the time, isn't it? Generic mugs all look the same. You made sure yours was completely different from anyone else's. So obviously yours. No possibility of getting it mixed up with theirs.'

Bill nodded. 'Yep. Some people had their own mugs, of course, but it made no difference. As long as I didn't do my own mug by accident, didn't get it mixed up with anyone else's, I was laughing.'

'Oi, Bill!' Charlie's voice boomed across the room. 'What you doing?'

Bill smiled. 'Hello, Charlie. Gracie, you remember Charlie, don't you? Come in, mate. You'll like this.'

The uniformed coppers in the doorway let Charlie through on a nod from Carter. Charlie barrelled in until Winslet stopped him with a hand on his chest. 'So, you this Jack fellah, then?' said Charlie.

'I am.'

Charlie threw his hands up. 'Right under me bleedin' nose, and I never saw it.' He glared at Bill. 'Lucky for you I never. I'd have torn your head off your scrawny little shoulders.'

Bill chuckled. 'Would you, Charlie? I doubt it. You have no idea, do you? *No* idea about what I've been doing in my room of a night. I've kept myself fit over the years, Charlie.

214

In my room. Locked the door. Did stretches. Mobility. Push-ups. Used my little TV as a makeshift weight. Aging doesn't always mean disaster, mate. Not if you prepare yourself in advance. *Well* in advance. In my game, fitness is everything. I mean, there are other factors that come into play. Genetics for one, and I seem to have been gifted with good genes. Strong genes. Lucky, I suppose.'

'Let her go, Bill. This ain't right. You know it.'

'Of course I do. It wasn't right when I captured and killed the others. It's clearly not about *right*, is it? And since when do you care about her? You hate her as much as me. I'm about to do you all a favour. You don't really want me to stop.'

'*I* do, Bill. Please don't.' Everybody turned to the new voice in the room. Susan stood in the doorway, wringing her hands across her body.

Bill loosened his grip. 'Tch. Oh, Susan, what are you doing here? I don't want you to see this. Not now.'

'Bill, please . . .' She stood next to Charlie. 'You don't have to do this. Not now. She's not a problem anymore, Bill. You got rid of her. She won't be back.'

Bill scoffed. 'I don't want to take that chance, love. She's a vindictive cow. She'll come for you. And Dunbar. And you too, Charlie. I can't let that happen. You're the only good people I've ever known. She has to go.'

There was sudden bang as the main doors of the building flew open and the sound of running feet filled the hallway. Bill looked toward the noise. He saw two men in full battle gear and carrying machine guns take up position in the doorway.

'Oops,' said Charlie, 'the big boys are here. Game over, Bill.'

'You!' shouted one of the men. 'Armed police! Release the hostage and put down your weapon. I am authorised to use deadly force!'

Bill laughed. 'Oh, right. Okay, then. If you say so, scary man. Er, no. Try your luck and she's dead. These two will tell you, my knife's already about two inches into her back.

215

You move, I push. Goodnight. And I know exactly what I'm doing. She'll be dead before I drop her. Your call, scary man.'

The gunman hesitated.

'Stand down!' Carter shouted. 'Do not fire. Repeat. Do not fire!'

The man lowered his weapon slowly.

'Good boy,' said Bill. 'Good boy.' He walked over to a chair that was half under a table. He hooked it out with his foot, dragged it toward him, manoeuvred it to where he wanted it and pulled the knife out of Draper's back. Carter was staring at the blood dripping from it.

Bill quickly pressed it to her throat, not hard enough to penetrate, but hard enough for those close enough to see the point make an indentation in her skin.

'Now . . .' he said. 'First of all, I want to say thank you to Susan here. And you, all you police officers, you should be thanking her too. Without her keen eye, her instincts and her willingness to do something, namely betray me, she managed to do what your lot couldn't do for fifty-odd years.' Susan had winced at the word *betray*. It was true, of course. Maybe she would never quite forgive herself for it. 'Susan, come here.' He beckoned her over.

Winslet stepped out in front of Susan as she started forward. 'Whoa! Whoa! Whoa! Stay there, Susan. You're not going anywhere near him.' She gazed defiantly at Bill. 'Not happening, Bill. You know I can't allow that.'

Bill glared at her. This was not the time to defy him. He turned his glare to Susan. 'I said, come here, Susan. I meant it. Now come here!'

Susan hesitated. Winslet still blocked her path. 'Stay there, Susan. Stay there.'

'Well, if you don't, I'll open up her throat and you coppers can do whatever you wish to me. But she will be gone. Gracie? Will you sacrifice Draper?'

Winslet hesitated. She was caught.

'Well, Gracie, my love? Will you sacrifice her? Will you? C'mon. Tick-tock, Gracie. Tick-bloody-tock.'

'I'm not giving you another hostage, Bill. No.'

Bill started a slow pull on the knife. Draper's eyes widened at the realisation of what he was doing.

Carter edged forward. Bill ignored him. He wouldn't dare. Not now.

'Okay! Okay!' yelled Susan. 'You win. Stop it, Bill! Just stop!' She was trembling.

Bill smiled and stopped. Winslet and Draper breathed a huge sigh of relief at the same time. Winslet's was louder.

Winslet looked at Susan. 'You don't have to do this.'

Susan nodded. She seemed different. Not so scared. More angry. 'I know I don't. I want to. I have to. You can see I do.'

Winslet looked nauseous as Susan made her way forward.

'Pull up a chair, Susan,' Bill said.

Charlie looked agitated, as if all of his East End protection instincts were switched on high. 'You touch her, Bill, and I will kill you with my bare hands. You understand me? I'll kill you stone dead.'

'I understand you, Charlie. I do. Thank you for the threat.'

Charlie watched anxiously as Susan stopped in front of the two of them.

'C'mon, Susan,' Bill said. 'Grab a chair and sit down. Next to Draper.'

Susan's expression changed. The fear was back.

'Come on,' said Bill. 'I won't hurt you. I promise. I'm going to show you something.'

'Give me that spoon there.' He pointed with his chin toward a small teaspoon. 'Yeah, that's it. That's the one.'

Susan handed it to him, handle first.

'Thank you. Now . . . hold on.' With a deft movement, he pushed the handle into Draper's ear. Deep. She screamed with the agony of it. Everyone instinctively moved to help the woman. Susan dropped her head and closed her eyes to blot out what was happening.

'Ah-ah! No, no! Back you go. Go on, all of you. Go on. Back.' Bill gestured with his chin again. They all stood down. Draper was sobbing, her face wracked in anguish. Blood from her ear dribbled down her face and jaw.

Bill stepped lightly and swiftly sideways, bringing the knife to Susan's throat. She froze.

'Bill . . . Please . . . Don't.' Tears streamed down Susan's cheeks.

The firearms officers jerked their weapons up to the ready position.

'This is for your sake, Susan. I'm going to give you some rules. Rules for life. For your future career. For if you ever interview people like me. Ready?'

She never moved.

'First . . . never volunteer for anything. If you do, you never know what's going to happen — like having a knife against your throat. Second . . . never, ever believe a serial killer when he tells you he won't hurt you. Third . . . never, ever get yourself into a dangerous position like this. Think clearly about the possibilities of your actions. Fourth . . . never, ever trust a serial killer when he's about to die.'

The gunmen took a few steps away from each other.

'Do you understand me, Susan?'

She whimpered.

'Do you?' His tone was firm. He wanted her to acknowledge him right now.

'Yes! Yes, Bill! I understand! I understand!'

Bill nodded. 'Good.' He suddenly took the knife away from Susan's throat, stepped back behind Draper and jammed the spoon deep into her ear. She screeched the screech of the banshees as the spoon broke bone and cartilage before burying itself deep in her brain. Her eyes bulged with terror and pain. Her mouth gaped wide and her jaw dropped at the hinge, as if someone had pushed a button. With his other hand, he drew the knife across her throat and, with a flourish, raised his arms wide as blood spurted from the throat of Jackie Draper. His last victim.

The gunmen hesitated for second.

In the same instant as Bill raised his hands, Susan leaped from her chair. She turned to Bill, her arms flailing at him. The gunmen opened fire. Two bullets hit her square in the back before the gunmen found their intended target.

Bill and Susan crashed to the ground together.

Winslet screamed. Carter bolted towards Susan. 'Get the ambulance crew in here! Now!' He dropped onto his knees into the puddle of blood that was seeping out of Susan's back. He rolled her over and looked into her eyes. The light was going out.

Charlie stumbled backward and crashed into a table before his legs failed him and he fell to the floor. 'Susan . . . Ah, no! No!'

Bill, flat on his back and with bullet holes in his chest and shoulder, rolled his head to the side, eyes filled with tears. His lips trembled as he let out a gurgled word. 'Susan . . .' Blood trickled from the corner of his mouth. 'I . . . I'm sorry,' he uttered. 'So . . . so . . . sorry.' Jack the Knife clenched his eyes shut, unable to take any more. The life that had been filled with fear and violence for over fifty years seeped away into nothingness.

'Where's the fucking ambulance crew!' Carter yelled. He stayed on his knees, holding Susan's hand.

Winslet, sobbing, held the other one. 'Come on, Susan. Stay here, hun. Stay with me, huh? We can get to know each other better. Girls' night out. Me and you? What do you say? Come on, Sue. Please. Please.'

Two paramedics burst into the room.

'Move! Move! Move!' one of them screamed as he dropped to his knees in front of Susan.

Carter, covered in blood, stood up on shaky legs and pointed at the other one. 'You keep her alive. You hear me? Keep her alive or else!'

He wandered over to Charlie and helped the old man to his feet. Charlie thanked him, pushed him away and headed for Bill. 'Charlie! What the . . .'

Charlie swung an almighty kick at Bill's dead face. 'You bastard! You evil, no-good bastard!' He kicked Bill's face again before Carter pulled him away.

'No, Charlie! He's gone. Leave it. Leave it!'

Charlie dropped himself heavily onto a chair and howled with grief.

CHAPTER FORTY-NINE

Eighteen days later, Bill's body was cremated. Nobody came to see him off. Nobody cared. Except the press. They were there to see his cheap coffin carried in by the pallbearers, whose faces gave nothing away. They knew their pictures would be all over the news. Not every day you got to carry a killer of this magnitude to the oven.

They hadn't been gentle with his remains at the funeral home. He was dropped into a box that was a foot too small. One man broke his legs at the knees and twisted them up beside his body. They slid his skinny, naked corpse into the back of a funeral car and sat in silence all the way to the crematorium.

Once they had carried him in, the vicar closed the doors to the gawking press. The men carried him down the aisle, not on their shoulders but by the handles, and shoved his cheap wooden coffin onto the platform. The vicar never bothered with a prayer. He couldn't bring himself to.

He stood on the hidden button behind his lectern and watched as Bill's coffin lowered into the fire. The pall bearers were already walking away.

* * *

Across town, two hundred people crammed into St Michael's crematorium and wept as Susan Johnson's body was lowered. For half an hour before, the vicar there had spoken of her childhood, her kindness, her selflessness and her belief and trust in the good of humanity. He spoke of her studies, her desire to be a forensic psychiatrist, another way to help her fellow man, and of her courage in bringing down Leonard Clifford, aka Bill Roach, aka Jack the Knife. And he paid tribute that she gave her life as she tried to stop him killing Jackie Draper. His service was sincere and fitting.

DS Winslet and DCI Carter, along with Carter's whole squad, took up the back two rows of seats. Winslet sobbed gently, a lump the size of a cricket ball blocking her throat. She found herself clutching Carter's hand as tears rolled down her face. Carter, too, struggled to contain his emotions. He sniffled several times. He needed a handkerchief but needed Winslet's hand more.

When the service ended, the mourners filed out of the crematorium and made their way into the gardens to look at the floral tributes and talk of the girl they knew and loved. Winslet couldn't bring herself to speak to Susan's mother and father. Not yet. They had been invited back to the house so maybe she would then. Just not now.

Packed against the gates were the press. They were out in force, desperate to catch a photograph of Susan's parents at the most painful moment in their lives. Anyone who lived or worked at the home would do: Mrs Dunbar, Charlie, Jenny Teach, anyone who saw something. Big money was on offer for the story. Excitement rose when they spied Winslet and Carter holding hands. It didn't matter that it was just two people supporting each other. This was good. This was news. The day wouldn't be a complete waste.

Behind the press was a hoard of local people. Some knew her, most didn't, but all had come to say goodbye to a local girl who had lost her life in trying to do yet another good thing.

Flowers were piled high against the wall, some tied to the railings, some laid by the side of the gates, far enough away from the stone pillars on which the gates hung to allow cars out.

Grace Winslet watched a man approach her and Carter and he squeezed Carter's hand. The man was in his fifties maybe. He was tall and dressed appropriately in black suit and black tie.

'Excuse me,' he said. 'Are you the police officers who were at the home when Susan died?' He had a northern accent.

Grace eyed him warily while Carter loosened his grip on her hand, ready to take this man down if he so much as made any kind of unwelcome move toward either of them.

'Maybe,' she said. 'Who wants to know? You press?'

'What? No. No, I assure you.' His voice was deep, his speech pattern fluid. Carter tightened his grip on Winslet's hand, clearly deeming this man to be non-threatening.

'I just wanted to say well done to you all, to the police officers who killed him. And I had to come and say goodbye to Susan, of course. God bless her. She seems to have been a lovely young girl. I wish I had met her.'

Grace was still wary. 'Okay, then. So, who are you? If you didn't know her, how did you get in?'

The man stared at her. 'Confidence, my dear. It's easy to go anywhere if people don't see you as a threat. My father taught me that.'

Grace froze. Carter let go of Winslet's hand and made a fist. He was more than ready now. Coiled, ready to strike. This time there was no hostage to think of.

'My father never taught me much, but he taught me that.' He nodded. 'And he also taught me a saying.' He looked at the two detectives. '*The apple doesn't fall far from the tree.* So, if you have time, I need to tell you about the things I've done.'

THE END

THE JOFFE BOOKS STORY

We began in 2014 when Jasper agreed to publish his mum's much-rejected romance novel and it became a bestseller.

Since then we've grown into the largest independent publisher in the UK. We're extremely proud to publish some of the very best writers in the world, including Joy Ellis, Faith Martin, Caro Ramsay, Helen Forrester, Simon Brett and Robert Goddard. Everyone at Joffe Books loves reading and we never forget that it all begins with the magic of an author telling a story.

We are proud to publish talented first-time authors, as well as established writers whose books we love introducing to a new generation of readers.

We have been shortlisted for Independent Publisher of the Year at the British Book Awards three times, in 2020, 2021 and 2022, and for the Diversity and Inclusivity Award at the Independent Publishing Awards in 2022.

We built this company with your help, and we love to hear from you, so please email us about absolutely anything bookish at feedback@joffebooks.com

If you want to receive free books every Friday and hear about all our new releases, join our mailing list: www.joffebooks.com/contact

And when you tell your friends about us, just remember: it's pronounced Joffe as in coffee or toffee!

ALSO BY STEVE PARKER

STANDALONES
JACK KNIFE

Milton Keynes UK
Ingram Content Group UK Ltd.
UKHW010624291123
433416UK00005B/363